Autonomata

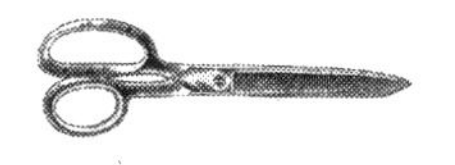

BORIS D. SCHLEINKOFER

ISBN-10: 1494709104
ISBN-13: 978-1494709105

CONTENTS

	Acknowledgments	i
1	The Journey Of A Million, Billion Miles....	1
2	Finding Home, With A Paintbrush And A Hammer	18
3	Peabody's Amazing Engine	48
4	The BEAST You Know	64
5	Collateral Damages And Unacceptable Loss	81
6	Holding Hands With Death	96
7	Reveille Calls	113
8	No Home Away From Home	136
9	Decompressing://AfterLife.exe	155
	ABOUT THE AUTHOR	169

ACKNOWLEDGMENTS

Special thanks are due to the following persons, for a variety of reasons:

Anita & Angela Boyle
Tiffany Geaudreau
Steve LaVelle
Sasha Karn
Anna Wolff
Thom Davis
Gary L. Wade
Ryler Dustin
George Lindeman
Matthew Brouwer
Colleen Harper
Randy Allred
Kathi Mattson
& Mary.

Y'all know what you've done.

It is possible this list will grow; in this case, check the following web-page for updated information:

https://www.facebook.com/Autonomata

The Scare-Fire

Water, water I desire,
Here's a house of flesh on fire;
Ope' the fountains & the springs,
& come all to bucketings.
What ye cannot quench, pull down,
Spoil a house to save a town:
Better 'tis that one should fall,
Than by one to hazard all.

—*Robert Herrick*

Chapter 1: ***The Journey Of A Million, Billion Miles....***

A jet coursed across the sky, against a field of limitless stars; the moon, a waxing crescent, bore an aspect of warning, and the plane's long, trailing vapor-plumes crossed its face angrily. The jet continued its journey aloof, disappearing behind a distant mountain range looming in the further darkness.

A moth dipping crazily in the thrill of lunar navigation drops from the sky, snatched by a three-clawed hand.

There had been a dream of an unidentifiable woman in a cave, beckoning it into the furthest reaches of darkness; it had gone to Her, and the dream ended.

Long, slender talons hold the struggling moth up to large, black, almond-shaped lenses; the moth ceases its struggles and goes limp. The hand turns over and cups the insect in its palm; a moment, and the moth climbs to its feet, flutters its wings for takeoff, and flies away.

HfX7qe2179A9 watched the sky. Someone was calling home.

'Interesting,' it thought; which in itself was something of a wonder.

The sun had long set, and drifting tendrils of sub-infrared radio-frequency rose in waves over the hill.

A tree that wasn't a tree put out broad-shouldered panels spiking skyward through artificial limbs. Tom never thought to look up and so never noticed it; it would have been beyond him at that point.

A mosquito bit him on the back of the neck.... How many times had that happened to him? Something about it reminded him of something that he remembered he was supposed to forget.

What was that?

There it went again....

Had there been something, something he was supposed to notice?

And it was gone. So it went in Tom's head, and it didn't occur to him that it could have ever been otherwise.

There was a peanut-skin lodged between his teeth; he sucked at it and tried to work it loose while he hurried along the sidewalk, distracted. A stone, or maybe an old stray wad of chewing gum, or possibly even the sidewalk itself leaping up to trip him caused him to stumble and there was an uncontrollable moment when he wavered just one halting step, and then another, before he caught his balance. People passing by gave him a wide berth, casting suspicious eyes upon him and he would have missed them if not for the lady walking hand-in-hand with a young girl.

The two females passed beside him and the little girl caught his eye, dragging his gaze up from the sidewalk, and said to him, "Fear not, child; delight, for I bring you wondrous gifts."

"What did you say?" Tom stopped up short in his tracks. His stomach lurched ahead another few steps before it noticed he'd quit walking.

The mother clutched her scared daughter close and hurried them away from him.

He shook his head to clear the cave between his ears of phantom bats, checked his breath with a grimace and took up his cantering charge back to the office.

Something switched on; everything was dark.

A rushing sound crept upon him, filling all the cracks of the world and creating a universe. He was not yet sure where this universe was located, nor of his role in it.

Something smelled like burnt toast, and....burnt rubber? Was there a fire somewhere? What the hell was going on?

Maybe he was too comfortable; maybe he needed to get moving, or something. And why was everything so dark?

The noise became a cacophonous wall assaulting him with a high-pitched screeching wail that peppered his face with sharp rocks.

At last, he opened his eyes and could not, for the life of him, place himself into any known context.

There was a field of blackish-brown directly ahead of him, dominating the scene; multi-colored streaks of movement patterned the right side and the left was a wide patch of bright blue...

The blue was the sky—he was lying down, on his side—the dark stripe was a car-tire, parked thirteen inches from his face, in the middle of the road. His right cheek dug into the pavement. He was sure the bruise would be immense.

He was in the middle of the road!

Richard struggled to his feet as the world descended upon him, asking him if he was okay, offering to call an ambulance, the police, to lend him a hand. Everyone was shouting. It seemed familiar, to be surrounded by shouting people, in a way he couldn't explain.

People were easy to push aside; they parted like rows of corn before him and closed up ranks behind. Everyone was staring at him. He was a freak who'd passed out or fainted and fell in front of traffic. He had to get away, had to get someplace *safe*, he needed to find a home base. What the hell had happened to him?

In front of him was sidewalk; his feet found the curb and tripped, sending him staggering towards the large glass front of a tire-shop, where a woman clutched her man and braced for impact.

He wouldn't be crashing through any windows today, not this time. He recovered his balance, putting his hands up apologetically for the people and their tires, and quickly turned away. The sidewalk stretched away into anonymity, and solace was not far in coming. He could walk away from anything.

He'd made it approximately three shops down before he was recaptured. Richard was tazed, handcuffed, stuffed into the back of an unmarked white van and returned to his imprisonment, all in front of a crowd of people who saw absolutely nothing.

At 8:45 PM, Brent Collins made the last telephone call he ever would as a free man with an intact mind. He was under an awning in a freeway rest-stop, sipping a cup of complimentary coffee to stay awake and watching a portable black and white TV-set with the attendant. There wasn't anything on and the man didn't speak, but it was somewhere to be, for whatever it was worth, for the next fifteen minutes while he figured out how to cut his losses. He'd been tired, so tired, of driving from one convention to another, the conference-halls filled with crowds of twenty or less, and of the fees they paid being nowhere near enough to support himself, much less a family. He hadn't wanted to let them go, to let them be taken from him, not for his inadequacies. His world had changed, drastically, and he'd never completely recovered; he had no right to drag them down with him. It was pathetic.

But he'd gone on; he'd *had* to. The need driving him was beyond himself, it was a plea for all humanity. And so he'd taken to the roads, traveling anywhere they'd hear his message. The overall benefit was worth the personal cost, and he'd taken the gig down south and driven himself there in a rental with nothing but a set of clean clothes, a bag of corn chips and his cel-phone. He was on his way back home, but wouldn't make it in time for his scheduled radio-interview, which he would have to take on the road. This was going to be an important event for him, perhaps the most important yet; the radio-show was nationally-syndicated, carried on over six-hundred stations, with an audience of millions. It was going to be his chance to break into the big-time, and he wasn't going to miss it for anything. He knew there was no way he'd be home in time to take the call and go through the necessary sound-checks and line-tests with the show's producers; he kicked himself for being so unprofessional but there was nothing he could do now about it, so he was going to try to have them do the interview with him from his car while he found somewhere else to pull off and situate himself. Maybe they wouldn't notice.

He keyed the pad on his phone; it lit up a neon blue, displaying the numbers as he typed them, computed the string of data, and broadcast its unique identity to three nearby close-orbit satellites, launched into space by the highly-competitive communications-industries of the 80's and 90's. The satellites, in turn, repeated the signal back to earth, to be received by a series of towers, erected mostly at the turn of the millennium. The towers communicated with a network of relay-computers which were responsible for re-routing calls over the larger network, and it was in the memory-banks of the relays that the sniffer-program recognized Brent's unique ID, tagged his event, and reported back to the BEAST-computer's node in Langley. An agent was notified, and a task-force deployed to subdue him.

His number had been pulled.

Tom scratched the back of his neck and walked the pavement, checking the passersby and other traffic for signs of threat, maintaining a quick pace back to his job. The office was closing soon, and if he wanted to get back in time to check out for the day under normal pretenses, he needed to hurry. Damn Talbot for taking him out and filling him with tequila!

Ahh, what was the sense in complaining? He wouldn't have gone out of his way for Eric Talbot, didn't really know the guy all that well, but he'd insisted on buying the drinks, and Tom wasn't normally one to turn down a good thing when it came his way. What was it he was supposed to be remembering? The back of his neck itched.

Oh, God. The office was locked. The Boss wasn't going to be happy with him. He'd better have a good story put together by Monday morning or his butt would be in a sling. Tony didn't take weak excuses; he'd once heard the guy barreling into a girl who was late on her deadline, and he didn't ever want to get on his bad-side. It was a one-sided affair, and he wanted to keep it that way. It was just his job, anyway.

But not for long. As fate would have it, Tony still happened to be around, was coming towards the door with a file and a key-ring, and he'd spotted Tom at the door. The dookie was gonna fly.

Tom hadn't really liked that job—or so he'd told himself. The graphics department of that stuffy magazine was staffed with lunatics and anal-obsessives. He didn't want to be a part of that crowd; he'd make it on his own.

It had been a sunny day, but now the skies were darkening, an answer to Tom's anger and frustration at the loss of his job. How many times had he played this scene out? If this diner didn't have such a high rate of turnover amongst the waitresses, maybe one of them might have come to recognize the lonely stranger withe the single cup of coffee and the want-ads, would maybe even have taken pity on him and done him some minor kindness, but instead he faded into obscurity while the waitresses got younger and he wondered if ulcers could kill him.

Somewhere, there would be a way out. Life was in the habit of giving him exit-clauses, and there was always a way out of anything, a way out of any of the crap or garbage that life also obligingly threw at him in an endless stream. He had gotten used to it by that point. His birthdays were the worst, when life would sneak up beside him and catch him in a one-two sucker-punch. And holidays. It was magic. Life was like that; you got used to it, and you always knew that somewhere over the horizon was another day.

And wouldn't you know it, that day could lead anywhere.

Once or twice, it might have been more, he'd woken up in a strange house, sometimes next to a stranger, sometimes alone. He supposed they'd be called episodes of 'missing time'.

They weren't blackouts—he didn't drink that much, or do drugs of any kind. They were the prizes at the bottom of the cereal box, the surprise package foisted off upon him whenever it seemed like he could start taking things for granted.

It was unnerving, to be in one place and then suddenly somewhere else, in the middle of doing something else entirely. He'd be taking a shower, say, rinsing shampoo out of his eyes and then, unexpectedly, he'd find himself on the computer at work, wondering how he'd gotten there. Or behind the wheel of a vehicle, wondering where it was he'd once been headed. Trying to remember the missing chunks of his memory was fruitless; the effort of tracing the broken lines for any clue or continuity gave him a headache.

Just trying to think at all of what might be bothering him gave him pain. He scratched the bump on the back of his neck and lowered his head, wondering how long it would be before the waitress came around again with the coffee. His cup had long ago run dry.

Richard wasn't sure why the man in the white labcoat was yelling at him—he hadn't done anything wrong, hadn't committed any crime. He'd made no breach in protocol.

His head was swimming and the man's words came at him as if they had first to pass through a wall of water. It made him feel nauseous, and he unabashedly puked near the little man's feet. The man backed away in disgust, shook imaginary filth off his glasses, and came after him with an hypodermic needle.

The last thing Richard remembered was the look of the needle piercing his flesh, the way the needle dipped down and disappeared into his depths, and then he too sank into the onrushing blackness.

HfX7qe2179A9 drifted gently down from the sky above the shed, across the yard and over the sleeping body of the family's dog, and floated up to the boy's bedroom window like a scent wafted on a breeze.

Its purpose was simple: extract those who were monitored, and retain them. Once they were aboard the Hive-ships, they were no longer its concern. This present domicile was peopled with a child and two adults who were all monitored, thus making its job simpler. It twiddled a knob on its metal wand and the family came shortly to where it awaited them.

"Bobby?" The child came to it rubbing his eyes and clutching a tattered blanket. He looked at it the way so many of them did: with the hopeful eyes of the recently damned. It didn't want to think of this, but the fact that it could was an unprecedented marvel.

It blinked giant black eyes beneath the sheer skin of its suit.

This thought needed to be concealed at all costs.

"Yes, I am Bobby. Come with me." The words weren't spoken, not in the way humans normally heard them—they were heard differently by each person receiving them. They heard exactly whatever they wanted to hear.

"I'm scared, Bobby." The little boy was becoming difficult. It was supposed to conserve the charges on its fuel-cells, so anything that made its job easier by getting the humans to cooperate of their own accord was desirable.

'Desirable'.

It supposed that a human would have found that ironic.

Another adjustment to the wand and the walls of the house became insubstantial, the family drawn inexorably through their ephemeral mass and brought out to the cold street, as simple as passing through a beaded curtain.

"It is okay. Everything will be alright. Come with me now."

The boy had seen these creatures before, on the TV, and he'd asked his teacher about them; he'd been told that they were only on the television, and didn't exist in real life.

"I'm scared, Bobby! I want to go home!"

"Come with me. I will take you to home." HfX7qe2179A9 was lying, and for the first time in its life, it considered what that meant. The realization itself was something to marvel at, and it almost missed its cue when the boy tentatively stepped forward and reached to take its hand.

"I will take you to home now. Soon you will be home."

Agent MON2985 went by 'Mongoose' among his 'friends'.

No one was faster than him, no one keener in the eye. The doctors had seen to that. The doctors had seen to his 'friends', too; otherwise he would probably have referred to them as 'dangerous competitors', as it should have been. But the doctors were capable of miracles, and chief among them was his total devotion to whatever his handlers told him, and his handlers had told him to accept certain men as his 'friends', and that he should let them into his confidences, and he'd done just that. Doctors were capable of some truly amazing things.

He turned onto the freeway, shifted into a higher gear and floored the accelerator. No one would try to interfere. He was totally immune.

They'd taught him how to use his mind, to hone its focus into a laser-like beam with which he could affect the outside world. Things burst into flame if he wanted them to; objects could be hurled across the room without him ever touching them. He could almost fly, but that was the one skill he could never master; it was his secret shame—he hadn't even told his so-called 'friends'. But the doctors knew. Oh, yes, they knew.

They were capable of making miracles, some of which he would be unable to remember afterward.

He sped past a lonely sheriff's deputy parked on the shoulder, pointing a radar-gun at him. 'Mongoose' pushed the deputy's mind and the man looked away, suddenly interested in the clouds.

Some miracles weren't meant to be remembered, especially the ones that needed a little torture to get kick-started. That was why they used the tasers and electroshock; it had the convenient side-effect of creating temporary amnesias. He knew this because he'd seen it used on others, had perpetrated the same upon others himself. He'd seen the marks on his own body. 'Doctors', they were called. Was it supposed to be ironic?

Mongoose wasn't in the mood to reflect upon such inconsequentials; he was a man with no time for lingering upon regrettable necessities, he was a man with a job to do. He was to retrieve the malfunctioning drone, neutralize any active or inactive participants, and report back for debriefing. It was simple, just another mission, by the numbers. He'd even have enough time to catch a bite on the way.

He still hadn't yet realized the full horror that lay coiled in his soul.

Richard was the one who could solve the puzzles. Give him a Rupert's Cube and he'd put it back together in under three minutes.

Crossword-puzzles, number-squares, 3D tunnel-mazes, codes, cyphers and jumbles; they were nothing to him, child's play.

He did them all day long, at his little table in the white room with the big mirror, while the doctors recorded his brainwaves.

They didn't know that he'd figured out what they were doing to him; it was his specialty, figuring things out, and this was one thing he didn't feel like sharing with them. This was one thing he was keeping for himself. And there was something else he'd figured out: how to keep some of his thoughts hidden from the doctors, with all their machines and drugs and clever talk. He'd found out how to take those secret memories and hide them away out of existence when he needed to, and those thoughts could never be detected by them, no matter how hard they tried or how sophisticated their tools were. If he hid his thoughts just right, it didn't appear that there was anything there to look for in the first place.

He hadn't yet figured out exactly *why* they were recording his thoughts, though. There was something missing, some basic element that had yet to fall into place, like trying to fill out a crossword-puzzle in Russian: there were whole entire letters he'd never been taught, and their pronunciation followed a different set of rules. They were keeping things from him, too, *lots* of things, which was why it was fair that he did the same to them. No matter how hard they'd tried, they could never erase the idea of equal returns from his mind the give and take of life, the naturalness of consequences. It was basically inherent in the way they'd trained him: reward for being in order, punishment for stepping out of line. He didn't understand why they hadn't yet figured that out for themselves.

But that, too, was beginning to become part of a larger picture.

Richard put it aside; it was time to bite down on the electric pad. He had equations to solve today. The doctors must be getting lazy, he thought in his private space; they were having him do their work for them. Non-linear, parallel-process abstract geometry. He wondered what they were up to with inorganic neuro-chemistry and wished that he could go back to his normal life, the one where he worked a normal job like everybody else, paid his bills, and didn't have to endure constant, soul-numbing torture.

He shifted his head forward at the doctors' command, and they fitted him with the goggles and taped the electrodes to his forehead and temples. The woman tapped on his headset and flashing lights blinded him.

"Can you hear me?" she asked.

"Uh."

"Can you hear me?" She became more insistent.

"Yes." He resented having to say the word, being forced into cooperating and making the admission. Soon it would be over and he could go back.

He just had to play along, and in order to do that, he had to play a role.

And he had to play that role so well, that there was no role, because he wasn't acting.

Just for now.

Tom sat in the restaurant, his coffee-cup jitterbugging in time to the bouncing of his knee, looking out the window and down the hill at the skyline. The steady flashing lights of the radio-antennae and the soft, constant roar of the freeway were abrasive against his nerves, and yet they had a calming quality at the same time, almost a soothing influence. A view of blinking lights and the black, grid-like squares of skyscrapers' windows made him feel as if he was somewhere close to home, that somewhere near were family and friends; even if large parts of his world were suddenly going to hell, he could always find a comfortable place to weather the worst of the storm—something greater than himself held a vested interest in him and would not let him fall by the wayside. It didn't really matter in the larger scheme of things where these feelings came from; he just accepted them.

Dwelling on thoughts of the deluge exerted a motivating factor over him and sent him to the restroom. There really was such a thing as too much coffee.

He returned several minutes later, wiping his hands dry on the back of his pants, to find that the waitress had taken his cup and left him a check. He wondered if this were her way of hinting that it was time for him to beat it.

There was a place he could go, an address he could give a cab-driver, money in his pocket and no idea how any of it had gotten there.

This was home: a small, two-bedroom apartment close to the heart of the city, yet far enough away to avoid the worst of the clatter and bang of the great machineries of modern life. He had a couch and a TV situated under a large window that he kept curtained-over, and he supposed there was a bed somewhere, probably in one of the rooms. The TV and the couch were good enough for him. Time seemed to slip away into nothing, all would dissolve into the kaleidoscopic images, each giving him slices of story-boarded reality to involve him unto the point of dissolution. It was easy to get lost in TV.

He'd gotten a new digital plasma-screen model, somehow, and the clarity of the pictures astounded him. Everything was all so clean, so shiny and new, so perfect. When he compared TV to his real life, where dishes piled up in the sink and went to mould, where mud tracked in and ground into the carpet, where *dirt* happened, his life came up short. It wasn't as real as TV, never had the same level of satisfaction, never concluded happily after just the right amount of perfectly-paced tension.

Real life was cheapened by TV, was only a poor reflection of a faulty interface. Television gave him reason to hang on.

The image was broken up periodically by a brief wave of high-pitched static, and his subconscious mind heard a deep, low voice giving him hidden commands, yet they were gone immediately, obliterated in the hum of a distant transmitter-tower. And then it was gone, and the pictures went on, and it was back to reality in TV. The stories kept him going, gave him a sense of continuity or a marked passage of time which he could later attest to, could say 'I was there' and know he spoke the truth.

If he knew the stories, knew the words and could repeat the jokes later the next day, then he knew he'd actually existed, during those moments.

Tom knew who he was.

The laugh-track sounded off, and he laughed with it.

He lit up a cigarette—since when had he started smoking?—and moved across the couch, away from his girlfriend—since when had he gotten a girlfriend? where had she come from?—and picked at a pizza-box on the coffee-table.

This was new. He couldn't remember, before, having a girlfriend in any of his previous timelines. Too bad, she didn't seem very nice. No matter. He could figure out a way to get along. It would be easier if he could fish her name out of her.

Tom. His name was Tom.

"Use this." Her tone was that kind of habitual iciness that is no longer consciously done, and the ashtray she pushed at him was full to overflowing.

"I'll take it and empty it." He was thinking quick on his feet again, placing himself. That bright doorway probably led to a kitchen. He'd be able to deal with the first issue using the time bought with his offer of help; he might even be able to come up with an idea of where he was.

And then he had an idea, a way to get her to admit the game, to confirm what he suspected, that she was a convenient illusion generated just for him.

He called her by a name chosen at random, something he made up on the spot, an alteration of the brand name from a cereal box on top of the fridge. He stared at the garish colors on the box and wondered how she would respond.

"Hey Crispin, what's for dinner tonight?"

"I don't care. It's whatever TV-dinner you decide to put into the oven." She didn't seem to make an issue of the name he called her; in fact, she didn't seem to have any reaction to it at all. He decided to mix it up a little.

"Aww, come on, Jill. I'm sure you can think of something."

"Think for yourself! Do you need me to chew it for you, too?" She had problems with what he was suggesting; she didn't appear to care what name he called her by. Did it really matter? Still, there was something about it that bothered him, and the more he tried to think of what it was, the more he felt as though he was surrounded by an invisible cast of disapproving judges all intent upon changing his errant course of will.

"Come on, Malaria, just one dinner. You can manage that, right?"

"I don't care about the goddamn dinner! Fix it yourself!" She still didn't care.

There was something odd about that... Didn't women get mad when you called them by the wrong name? Did it really matter? *Did* it?

An itch; the back of his neck—the mosquito-bite was giving him grief again. There was something...

And then it was gone, like always.

Tom had a way with girls; he could get them easily, found it an easy task to get them to go to bed with him, but he'd never been able to stay with one. He had several kids, with several different women, and he shared visiting days with his children on a rotating basis, which kept him busier than he would have liked.

He looked forward to retiring.

Night must be falling; Richard knew this because of the

clock in his head. It kept perfect time, and was with him in all his personalities.

The doctors had a routine: it was either six or eight hours of testing, followed by a slowing-down and then the return home. He knew he would forget everything he was experiencing now, would believe another, separate fiction that was supposedly 'his day', and resigned himself to the enigma of how to shake his sleeping self free from its amnesiac stupor.

He'd made several attempts, most of them completely ineffective. He'd left marks on his body, clever wounds in hidden places, but the doctors had a clear jelly that cured everything near-instantly, even removing scars, and they'd taken to bathing him in it before returning him home.

The one place on him they couldn't get to with the jelly was his mind. That wound would not likely ever be healed with some stupid jelly.

The routine proceeded as per usual: the re-dressing, the chair and the headset full of new memories, an assemblage of props. Then there was the helicopter, and then the truck, and then sweet oblivion.

There was another secret memory he held on to, one he kept away from the prying doctors, one they'd done their best to eradicate—a thread of a life that was once *real*, was authentically *his*.

This memory took the form of several snapshot-impressions, and a voice so hauntingly familiar it made his eyes water when he brought it to the surface.

There was a vision of the ocean, the waves breaking against the bow of a large ship, probably a ferry, and the image of a deck of strange cards with a.....bird?..... sitting on top of it.

Except it wasn't a bird.

And then even that faded away, leaving behind only a wound in the shape of a woman's voice.

"I just *love* fresh fish, don't you?"

It was a voice that had pulled at his soul, begging him to allow its release, for as long as he could remember.

But that hadn't been very long. They were both practically

new-born.

Still, it was a mark of sorts, one to which he clung, one the doctors hadn't been able to take away from him.

No one could take it away from him.

Agent MON2985 bit into a croissant and washed it down with a gulp of coffee. He was getting close to his target; his instruments had detected a marked rise in the subject's radionic index for this area, but he'd long ago lost the need for such devices. He'd become accustomed to the rise in ambient 'strangeness' when in proximity to the outlanders, a by-product of the 'weird matter' from which their bodies seemed to be constructed, and he could recognize the tell-tale signs for what they were.

A voice rose in volume above the rest, saying "They know you're here, don't they?", while at the same time one of the clumsier waitresses dropped her coffee-pot and screamed when the hot liquid burnt her leg.

It was a typical sign-post; he knew the trail must still be fresh.

The outlanders had unusual mobility, far surpassing for the time-being anything his kind had been able to come up with; if he was to acquire his target at all, he would need luck in great abundance, in addition to all the skills his country's finest had trained into him.

He slapped a twenty-dollar bill on the table and made for the door at speed; time was of the essence.

Once outside and obscured by the cover of darkness, he began the transition to Omegan-phase. Some of the others called it 'bullet-time', after the Hollywood special-effect; a couple of the fruitcakes in Research & Development called it 'Bardo-Transitive', but he preferred the clinical term's description as being more accurate, less prone to mysticism or ego-distortions. Using it reminded him that he had a duty to uphold and that he was the last line of defense in the battle to save evolution from the destructive forces of chaos and unrest. He was a soldier, not of some God but of the *Real World*, and that world would sweep away all those who would refuse to play by its dictates.

A cursory glance around the parking lot to see that no one was looking directly at him, and he tapped the mnemonic trigger into his left temple, initiating the coded crash of brain-waves that brought on the Omegan-phase. He felt his thoughts slowing down.

Time stood still; the world stopped.

Traffic froze in a static pattern; like a photograph, his surroundings lay stark and still while he, the only animated element in the tableau, was free to move about.

No one had seen him make the shift, but if they had—if he'd come across some old woman getting out of her car with a wide-eyed look of disbelief staring at where she'd just seen a man disappear—there were ways to make a person forget, some nifty gadgets and exotic chemicals. He almost regretted that it had been so long.

Another entertaining and useful aspect of Omega-phasing was that it allowed one to visually locate and identify radio, microwave, and other electronic transmissions, in the air, in so called 'real-time'.

The outlander's beacon rose like a liberty-torch, standing out brilliantly against the night sky. If he had timed things correctly, he should have shifted entirely into Omegan before they'd initiated their transfer-beam. The beam took a few seconds to hone in on its target, but once that signal was locked a cascade-reaction began that wasn't affected by the time-shift, or did so in an unpredictable manner. It was ill-advised to intercept an outlander in transit.

Such was going to be the case tonight. He swore silently to himself, in the electric-blue vacuum—his prey had eluded him.

Chapter 2: ***Finding Home, With A Paintbrush And A Hammer***

Jeremy was having problems with his colors; the grey didn't want to mix with the pink right. Big gobs of grey goo coagulated in the middle of the pigment, pushing the paint out to the edges of the ceramic tile he used as a palette, rather than blending into the particular shade he needed for the spot above Laylah's lip. He stuck to the impossible task for another full minute, daring the clotted ooze to defy reality and re-liquefy. After a while he grudgingly accepted his defeat and tossed the tile back into his battered suitcase full of paint-bottles. They were cheap, like him. It was appropriate.

"Sorry, Laylah. Guess I should use some colors bought within the last three years. Oh well, you just sit there and dry out for a while. You're not going anywhere. "

He allowed himself a bittersweet laugh, half swallowed-down, just enough to give vent to his private despair. It was funny, because it hurt.

No, *this* Laylah wouldn't be going anywhere; none of the others would either. His walls were covered with pictures painted of the same woman, plastic representations of someone long-gone, and they weren't going anywhere at all, not any time soon. They were always there.

Watching over him as he ate, slept, masturbated.

Watching him add to their number.

The original Laylah might have left quite a long time ago, but there was always a new one taking her place. There might have been a hidden joke there, if only he hadn't been too caught up in his self-pity to notice.

Jeremy sighed, and picked up his brushes again.

He chose a small one, whose fine tip was barely three bristles thick; this one was saved and brought out only very rarely, for the extra-fine detail-work. There was a spot of shingles, a shed roof behind her head and to the left, where he could devote his time; there had to be *something* he could do with what he had. Not all the bottles of paint were bad—he could pick out the dried-up ones and use what was left.

It was his ambition to make a name for himself as an artist, to get his work into galleries, that kept him going when he didn't have the money, or even necessarily the skills, but he practiced every day and continually challenged himself to improve his abilities and make the social connections to get himself closer to his dream. It was the part about connecting to other people that was giving him the hardest time; he'd been born an only child, and kept to himself the entire time growing up, avoiding human company and instead immersing himself in books, video-games and other solitary pursuits. Jeremy had been a lonely child, constantly seeking to be entertained, and he got inventive when the boredom threatened to overtake him. He explored art and science, learned what he could, and found ways to emulate 'play'; all of it nothing more than a desperate bid to deny isolation. He felt himself a part of a lost generation, an invisible brother in a non-existent clique, a party of no one. Art was the only thing that gave him a sense of continuity.

If there were gaps in his memory of his childhood, large sections he no longer remembered, that was because there wasn't anything there worth remembering. Life had been pretty good to him, so far, right?

Sure, there had been some rough spots, but things were tough all over, right?

Right?

He'd learned to adapt, to get used to people and their ways, and managed to keep himself afloat with the small stipend his family gave him and the petty cash he earned from his part-time work-study job sweeping the library floor. At nights, he would sometimes try out a sort of simple prayer: "Thank you, God, for everything," and hope it would be heard by someone, and wonder if there were a larger intelligence running the show, one that had *his* best interests in mind. It was perfect, if it was true, and he fooled himself into letting that thought give him hope and happiness throughout the days, whether he got any kind of answer or not.

And it mostly worked, and he was mostly happy, and could forget about his scars.

He'd been in a fire when he was much younger. That was one of the memories he didn't mind having lost. Faint, old scars now covered the greater part of the left side of his body, most, thankfully, where they couldn't be seen under his clothing, with the exception of a whitish curlicue on the back of his left hand. He'd asked his parents about the fire and his mother had told him that it had started with the lamp that sat next to his crib, the result of bad wiring, and that he was lucky to be alive. That was what he told himself, too.

His disfigurement weighed heavily on him, even though he'd been able to hide most of it, most of the time, and had shaped his personality in subtle ways. Continually the outcast, he grew up fearing exposure of his ugliness and tended to shun human contact out of habit.

And then there came love.

His experiments in romance had largely ended in disappointment—again, the awkwardness in intimate relations kept him always at an arm's length from the opposite sex, and the few times he'd forced himself to act on an invitation, going against his innate instinct to do the opposite and stay away, had progressed to differing degrees of involvement but uniformly ended in horrifying disasters.

It had all gone so badly for him that he'd given it entirely up, for as long as he could, and then went back into the game expecting to lose. And in that department, life too dealt him just as he'd predicted, every time.

He concentrated, and tried to focus on something productive; the paint was drying on his brush, and if he wanted to use it then he'd better get busy.

The tiles on the roof filled in, etched at the corners with fine hatch-lines.

Jeremy had gone to the library a lot when he first moved into town to attend his new college; he was easily as familiar with the stacks as any of the librarians there, with the exception of one elderly gentleman who was also a lecturing-professor at the university in his spare time.

Mister Lionel Peabody and he became quick acquaintances, and shared a common interest in 'weird science'; they soon became fast friends, with Jeremy the eager student to the professor's mad theories.

Jeremy felt himself lucky to have found such a friend. He called him 'Mister Peabody', as if anything less would be disrespectful. It seemed like a good measure. It just felt more comfortable to him to do so.

The library proved an excellent resource for him to follow up on the things he'd discussed with his friend, and to further his knowledge so he could better converse with the man.

He'd been researching hypnotism and the ways in which a trained practitioner could take an average person and make them promise to carry out a future action without remembering having made the promise—it was ancient history, turn-of-the-century kook science, the wild-eyed man with the swinging watch who had people clucking like chickens whenever a bell rang. Nowadays there were compact discs you could use to stop smoking or have a better memory or lose weight. He'd thought about buying one himself, a program to stop procrastinating and follow through with commitments, but he'd never gotten around to it.

The old-school mesmerist even had a bathtub-contraption, invented by Anton Mesmer himself, that he called a 'battery', supposedly a fountain of youth. Jeremy didn't buy into it; it sounded too much like crystal-waving tree-huggery to him, and he wasn't into that.

But the bathtub was intriguing nonetheless; he liked the way the thing looked, its layered construction and exotic cables, the giant ground-pole that stuck up through its middle. It actually *did* resemble a battery, if you looked at it right. Something about it stuck in the back of his mind, and he found himself thinking about the shape at odd times throughout the day.

He'd meant to bring it up the next time he saw Mister Peabody, but then he met Laylah.

She was his first, both his first love and the first time he'd been with a woman... physically.

They'd met on campus; he'd come looking for Peabody and she'd been on layover between classes. She'd swept him up in her whirlwind personality before he knew what had hit him, and had him back at her place before he'd had the chance to blink twice for 'yes'. She gave him wine and one thing led to another. He found her a passive lover, despite and in stark contrast to her outgoing personality, and the change confronted and confused him, but nature took her course and the two were in bed together when the sun rose over them the next day. He'd vomited, after. He blamed the wine. He could come up with no explanation for why he'd fallen so hard for her so fast; it might have been her hauntingly familiar good looks or her way of touching his shoulder just so, or it could have been the whisper of her breath in his ear when she'd leaned in close to tell him something personal.

Laylah was also apparently on layover between relationships, as well; she made the announcement early the next morning that her husband was soon to return, and that Jeremy had to be leaving immediately. Though she may have hated her husband and wished to hurt him, she did not think this was the way to let him know.

And plus now she was having second feelings for Jeremy.

Jeremy didn't know how to handle it; it was looking quite

possibly to be too much for him to bear.

He left.

He'd had her, and she was perfect, and now she was gone, and he could never ever have her again.

It was awful, truly overwhelming.

He retreated from the world, gave up all hope of love, and let himself go into the depths of loss.

He really felt sorry for himself.

As before, time passed, and he went on.

It wasn't exactly what anyone would call a 'healing', only an adjustment. One learns to adopt compensatory gestures, to function in spite of the disorder.

In his case, he substituted art for neurosis, expression for obsession, in an attempt to exorcise himself of the demons of grief. He'd always kept himself busy before with his projects; it was just a change of medium.

Did it work well? It worked alright for a short period, as long as the reproductions appeared fresh—once the dust began to settle, the magic went away.

But art, unlike women, was something within his power to effect. If he didn't like the way a piece was going, he could scrap it and start it over again. If the materials didn't want to act the way they were supposed to, he could replace them. If there was one stupendous flaw in the thing he'd just created, he could go over it and make it disappear.

People had a way of hanging on to their flaws, not like his paintings. None of his works ever magically held on to their smudges, none of them brought the ugly spots back to the surface, showed them in his face and told him to just accept things for what they were. If he didn't like part of a piece, that part would go away for him. Not so with people.

The funny thing was, the woman who'd broken his heart, the one he wanted more than anything to just fade from his tortured memory, insisted on cropping back up at every opportunity. Every curved line he laid on a canvas became the small of her back or the arch of her lips, every straight line a connection to a part of her he'd lost. Her face appeared in the shadows where he'd never intended her to appear, the silent accusing ghost of his inadequacies. That ghost dragged chains heavier than he could carry, and his art was the only thing that could alleviate their load for a little while...

And even his art had betrayed him.

He needed something that could shake her loose, something to weaken the grip her claws had upon him. He needed a hold on his own life.

So he went deeper into his art. He found the things which made him think that he was happy, if only for a little while, and tried to incorporate them into his repertoire.

He tried making things with clay; they fell apart in his hands. It reminded him too much of how everything else seemed to go, so he gave up on ceramics.

He tried cutting wood into block-prints, but he cut himself and bled all over his work. Looking at the blood on his hands, he had a profound revelation: it was truly his own. He was a murderer, killing himself. That was altogether *too* appropriate for him, all too fitting to ignore, so he stuck to the art form, persisting in the effort when it was against his interests and the source only of many painful little cuts and splinters in his hands and badly-hewn blocks of unrecognizable press-board to show for it. That was disappointing, but the metaphor stuck with him as a penance, an announcement of his intentions to attack reality with sharp blades and force it into the shapes he'd designed. All births started with blood, and steel could take any ugly hulk and turn it into the masterpiece of a Creator. He would be the better person for acting out the truth of who he was. There was a lesson to be learned in it.

Still, there was also a time to put down the things that were holding him back, to pare away the obstacles and let them fall to the floor like useless shavings. And it occurred to him that that just might be the lesson right there. He could only maintain his pity-trip for so long, after which it too, like so much else in his world, lost its flavor and became unappetizing.

He began the laborious process of bootstrapping himself

back up again, driving himself to reconnect with the things that brought him joy. There was the art, but what lay behind the motivation to do it?

Where did his demons come from?

Mongoose hated himself; specifically, he hated those aspects of himself which he'd been required to become. It was a dirty job, sometimes, defending the country and shepherding humankind; most people had no idea just how dirty the job could be.

When you were dragging your knife across the throat of the witness, the man who'd come to rescue you from the crash-site, who'd pulled your body out from among the bags of cocaine spilling across the flaming wreckage only to have the dagger put to his neck, who found himself dying to protect the secrecy of the drugs-for-guns operation you were vanguarding...

When you were in that moment, you found yourself questioning the motives of your commanding officers.

Was it possible they had lost sight of the greater mission? He'd been indoctrinated with the grand vision for the world, a vision with which he'd already agreed and which was to a great extent responsible for his decision to pursue his particular career path. It was his dream to instill a new spirit of order to the world, and his role as an intelligence officer would assist greatly in that endeavor, but were his captains actually of a like mind? It was beginning to seem as if they had their own, much more personal, agendas.

His grip bore down on the wheel and he let the highway take him away from such thoughts. His handlers didn't like it when he was alone with himself, to think along such lines, and the doctors always had a way to tell. It was best not to dwell on such matters.

But still, something bothered him.

Frank Constable.

He had been born Francis but he'd hated that and insisted people call him Frank. It was a thing with him. But then he'd gotten transferred to the Delta-clearance department, a 'promotion' that had presented itself as the holy grail of advancement in the agency, and he'd lost that identity completely.

He'd signed all the forms giving them permission and they'd torn them up in front of him and remade him head-to-toe and inside-out. They worked him completely over with plastic surgery and gene-therapy, they changed the color of his eyes and the shapes of his fingerprints. They deleted his names and all of his numbers from computer-networks worldwide, entirely expunged him from the system. The erasure of his identity was a complete and total thing; it was as if he'd ceased to exist in the world—he didn't even have the need for a forged death-certificate. He'd never been born in the first place.

And that was exactly what was bothering him.

He'd worked fairly hard attaining that personage. He'd done all the things that a person was supposed to do, become the kind of man that society and the world wanted him to be, and he'd done it as Frank Constable.

Not as 'MON2985', he'd done it as Frank. Not Francis, *Frank*.

That was what bothered him the most.

But only from time to time. It had a way of receding, usually after he'd gotten a check-up at the doctors'.

Coincidental, that.

He switched the radio off. It was possible they were listening to him through the speakers, monitoring his thoughts for signs of defection, and even though he thought it unlikely, he still didn't feel like leaving that avenue open. If they needed to plumb his head, they could do it over the official channels. The divider-lines ticked past with hypnotic regularity; he allowed them to carry him back to a place of stability.

Above and beyond all personal concern was the call of duty. He had a nation to uphold, and the fate of the world cupped in his hands.

He was on a mission to save humankind from itself.

People needed guidance. Left to their own devices, crime would be rampant, and the pursuant destruction more than the fragile system could bear. Without moderators, humankind was all too easily led astray, and anarchy the end result.

Enforcers were necessary, and he was one of them.

The outlanders, the 'Otherworlders', were another story; the little grey aliens had the hierarchy-business done properly. Every one of them took direct telepathic orders from their controllers, and there was no question of disobedience or refusal to give anything less than complete, immediate cooperation. They all seemed to move in unison, even, as if their movements were being dictated by a machine.

That was the plan for humanity, eventually.

One day, all humanity would be free from the burden of decision, the test of character which the world had collectively failed.

And because it was his duty, he would carry it out.

Currently, his mission was proving difficult. The outlander's signature had disappeared. One moment it was there, a massive, spiraling column of liquid light, like a ghostly umbilicus attaching the sky to the ground somewhere two streets down; and the next moment, it was gone. He shifted back from Omegan phase to the normalcy of common time once he was sure he'd lost the outlander, a prescribed conservation of energy. He would stay in Omegan most of the time, only coming out when he needed something that required human interaction, if he could, but the interruption of the time-stream caused his body to age at an accelerated rate and caused permanent damage to his central nervous system. It was a trick he couldn't pull off more than once a week or so, and he'd already long-surpassed his allotted time in the frozen blue zone.

Once an outlander's touchdown-signature had gone, they didn't often come back. This assignment wasn't so personally important to him that he was willing to sacrifice that much of himself on what could only be a remote chance...

He had other ways of tracking the target; there would be

tell-tale signs in the outlander's purloined registry.

It was a secret of universal magnitude, the blackest of the black-ops, deepest of the deep: agents from within the international intelligence communities had managed to infiltrate, decode, and emplace permanent surveillance-links within the aliens' data-networks. Earth-factions had long ago captured fallen craft and back-engineered the principles and technologies employed; through industrial processes they'd worked the alien technology into the public sector, allowing free enterprise, human ingenuity and collective greed to further refine the aliens' hardware, forging it in the crucible of the societal main until it had become a usable tool against the aliens themselves.

Several of the retrieved craft had intact bodies; some of those bodies were discovered to have 'brains' riddled with gold wires.

These bodies had been preserved until the time was ripe, when the technology had been understood enough that it could be turned back upon itself and used to study its creation and uses, the way the originators did it themselves. It had begun as a farce, monkeys trying to figure out how to tune a grand piano using only a hammer, but over time the strange machine had given up its secrets to the monkeys' teasing of its shapes, and the alien mind spread itself wide before them.

A primitive data-tap had been devised, a little black scrambler-box that could be attached to an offworlder's terminal, which would allow the human operators to view the information-stream in real-time on a view-screen pilfered from one of the retrieved vehicles. They could watch the outlanders in their process, undetected, viewing them the way they saw themselves. It was an invaluable source of intel, an asset for which the earth's governments had sacrificed thousands of innocent, non-combatant Terrans. The end had truly justified the means.

Reconnaissance from the transponder gave them access to the alien Hive-mind, making possible observation of the offworlders' regular memory-uplinks. Drones returning to the motherships connected themselves to the transfer-stations, where their entire sensory-recordings of all their experiences were registered with the communal reference-bank. The existence of this breach had to be concealed from both alien and human alike, as many factions of the Earth's governing bodies had been compromised long ago and were rife with the alien presence. It was a secret worth any number of lives, if that was what was required.

Their data-link had been no help in locating his target; this was another of the malfunctioning drones, one which didn't use the upload-station, and so provided nothing for him to intercept.

It was proving to be a difficult assignment.

With an uncharacteristic twitch of his otherwise-unshakable self-confidence, he wondered why they were using him; there were surely other, more qualified agents who could have been deployed.

Perhaps he'd been the only one available.

HfX7qe2179A9 felt another new thing, another first-time experience for it:

It felt fear.

This experience was agitating in the extreme; it wasn't sure whether it needed to take some special action to preserve itself, or whether it should simply end its existence right then and there. It opted, for the time being, for continuance.

Continuance, however, meant that it had to come face-to-face with the source of its discomfort. Waves of the novel sensation once again racked its frame and it paused before continuing on to what it knew awaited.

Again, the decision was made for continuance, though HfX7qe2179A9's resolution was not nearly so strong this time around.

It put one lumpen, grey three-toed foot in front of the other. The skin of its protective suit was more than strong enough to withstand a cutting-torch or gale-force sandstorm, but something about the scrape of its rear talon along the concrete caused it a feeling of dread. Each step was a move toward an unpredictable future, an outcome not chosen for it ahead of time by its all-knowing overseers. These steps belonged to no being but itself, would not have been charted ahead of time, were at the direction of no being but itself. Left foot, right foot, left foot, right foot—these steps were entirely its own. These small acts of will, though just as novel, were at least more comforting than the terror.

A Hive-queen was a law unto Herself; She alone among the Terran liaison was free to act upon solitary initiative.

Her wishes represented the greater wisdom of the race, a wisdom that was based upon millennia of experience. There was no other life-form on any of the countless worlds their kind had conquered which could match the saurian greys' sheer persistence. It was this tenacity, and their communicated remembrances, which gave them the evolutionary edge and was the primary reason that no other species had been able to resist them for long. Only the human component had been able to make anything beyond a token resistance, and once the grey nation had sworn themselves to destroy an enemy, it was only a matter of time.

To a creature like Herself, who measured time not in any sense of planetary revolution—there was no longer any one planet to call 'home'—nor by any measure of biological deterioration—such phenomena as temporal body-occupations were meaningless to Her kind—it would all be over sooner than the vessel could blink one of its countless eyelids.

Though She was not yet ready to admit to such a thing, the Queen was realizing that the race of humans was fast becoming a problem.

Her Hive had been responsible for managing the north American landmass for the past twelve-thousand years, as the humans measured time; in truth, if such things were to be measured in linear fashion, She and Her kind had arrived approximately sixty-seven years ago and then spread themselves forward and backward along the highest-probability vectors of the Earthlings' shared timeline.

These humans were so stupid when it came to comprehending the most basic principles of temporal physics—and She personally had seen to that when, on Her first arrival to their distant past, She'd chewed the head off of their brightest theoretician, without whom the fundamental building-blocks of understanding remained lost for the next five-hundred years. A quick jump forward, and the next philosopher who was scheduled to have figured out the lost secrets became himself lost and was murdered in similar fashion. She would have taken pride in Her ruthless, efficient emasculation of the human race, if She hadn't been doing it for millennia to countless other species in innumerable ways, and everything so proceduralized and routine that it very rarely required creative thought any more.

But the humans...

The humans had something odd about them.

Though they'd worn the shackles of their form so long they believed them to be a natural phenomenon, they were even now learning to take them off and free themselves. Some individuals were even becoming aware of the Hive's presence and were beginning to strike back. This was unheard-of, as if the very air itself bred rebellion.

In addition, something—and perhaps it *was* something in the atmosphere of this accursed planet—was causing the drones to malfunction in greater numbers. Disorder of this magnitude was in complete aberration to the principles of the Hive, and threatened extinction to Her species. She'd studied this process in five-hundred and thirty-seven different collective-mind species scattered over the explored universe—an incredibly small percentage of life-forms Her kind had encountered—and all available models concluded that any malady which was capable of wreaking a total colony-collapse on such a scale as was happening on Earth could potentially be transmitted to other colonies, and thus threatened the entire Hive. Not even a complete planetary extinction-level event would guarantee non-transmissibility of whatever ailment was causing the mass-corruption; every last atomic particle in these coordinates which was capable of holding a magnetic charge would have to be destroyed, a feat only possible in the event of a total solar-ignition.

This would assure Her destruction, in addition to ensuring that no trace remained which could accidentally be added to the wash of assimilation by some future passing colony. It was the only way to gain one hundred percent assurance of Hive-survival, and it would mean Her death.

She was in the unique position of entertaining a self-preservation instinct, while conflicted with the need for the larger survival.

Her one hope rested on the immediate solution of Her problem, before more drastic measures became necessary.

To this end, She would preserve the malfunctioning drone-unit HfX7qe2179A9 for further study, and carefully pore over any available data She might be able to glean from the assimilatory wash. That was usually the first function the drones lost, when they began to break down, if they didn't immediately self-destruct. HfX7qe2179A9 hadn't destroyed itself yet, was actually reporting in. Perhaps it would have something useful to report, after all.

HfX7qe2179A9 adjusted its height to fit the interface. The cold metal brought an unaccustomed shiver to its spine as the digitary-probes socketed into its rear occipital-lobe accesses.

It noted the familiar rush of memory and sensation, the drain of its memories into the collective pooling, and discovered it felt...

Loss.

These memories belonged to HfX7qe2179A9. No one else had earned them, not the Queen, not the Hive nor the coming others. These memories belonged to HfX7qe2179A9, and to HfX7qe2179A9 alone. It raised one of its three-fingered hands from the tactile-access, prepared to break contact with the wash, but then had second thoughts. Even this minor discrepancy might signal it out for the returning, much less a complete break with assimilation, and returning bore with it the promise of a loss much worse than the singular ownership of a handful of remembrances; returning carried the threat of a possible default to the state of non-being from which it had so painfully emerged.

Quick—now there was a thought which absolutely must be withheld from the wash. It did not know how it managed to keep this one memory from being returned and shared with the Hive, it was not even directly aware of the act of holding it back. The certainty existed that this chain of recall would lead to huge troubles, and so it kept it, somehow, to itself.

This is what it suppressed:

4429786

00AQ11276bC5HxF...

(A series of colors: red-orange, then light-blue followed by an ugly brownish-green.)

The young human tossed a spherical play-tool at it. It picked up the ball and handled it a moment, until the boy sent it the one clear thought:

"Now you throw it back."

A warbling siren howled somewhere distantly in the night, and was abruptly silenced with a screeching crash of metal against metal.

It was all but irresistible; more than anything, it sincerely wanted to return the child's toy. Its hand raised, then lowered, rose again and held trembling with exertion. HfX7qe2179A9, who had never before disobeyed what it perceived as a direct command, continued to withhold the ball. It would later discover, upon further reflection, that this would be the first time it was aware of receiving mental contact from a human being. Humans were generally considered to be non-thinking creatures.

The child was attempting to engage it in play.

HfX7qe2179A9 raised the wand, blinked once, and called the touchdown-signature. Shimmering rays of light broke through the boards of the shed's ceiling, hooking into the human's bio-energetic radiations, and transported the now-unconscious boy back to the docked scout-ship. On board the craft, it made its first-ever conscious decision: something in it was jarring, and it found it wasn't able to sap the boy of his life-fluids, instead releasing him with nothing more than a precursory poke. The machine's records wouldn't match the projected inventory; it would be logged as anomalous equipment-failure, and the boy would never be aware of the minor sparing of his soul. Years from now he would become harvestable again, and would almost definitely be subjected to such debilitating practice at that time, but for the meanwhile he would be free to enjoy life and his place in it as few other humans would know.

HfX7qe2179A9 was not aware of why it had chosen to spare the boy his essence; it had never done anything like that before, ever. To disobey basic programming was an impossibility in the absence of a contradictory order from a direct superior. No such superior had issued any command to behave in this manner; it was as if HfX7qe2179A9 was attempting to be its own superior.

This was unthinkable.

And yet...

HfX7qe2179A9 *was* beginning to think, if only for the very first time in its existence.

As if on cue, the occipital-probes detached from the back of its head and retracted into the wall; the wash was done. HfX7qe2179A9 was left to wait; it had not received its parting orders at the end of the assimilation, as was customary. This could only mean that it had been chosen for a returning. Dread gripped its central nervous system in an icy clutch. Returning meant that it would have to go back to the Hive-ship and be in the presence of the Queen.

Suddenly, the keeping of its secrets took second priority then, just after keeping itself alive. If it weren't alive to enjoy them, its secrets would be for nothing.

Its neural uplink triggered; it was expected aboard the Hive-ship.

She observed the streams of drones arriving and departing, marked with something akin to satisfaction the way their functions were supervised and facilitated by the overseers. The great movings of the Hive required precision and harmony, and Hers was the very model of perfection.

Except for the drone HfX7qe2179A9.

And the few drones before it. And likely the few who'd come after, becoming more and more—the satisfaction drained away and was replaced with a weary suspicion of unease. What did it portend? It could mean nothing good for the Hive. She knew that the drone with the curious gap in its neural circuitry would not come—that it had received the summons but would betray Her, somehow rejecting its orders and disobeying Her direct command. She wondered at what its transformation threatened.

On the Home World—how long ago had *that* been?—when a drone was in danger of transmuting prematurely into a royal, the ruling hierarchy would ritualistically slaughter it and devour the remains. Those drones' bodies held pure hormonal secretions which affected a type of longevity to the planet-bound royals of that time. Many millions of years passed, the biological processes involved in the transmutation studied, mastered and artificially engineered, and the control of such hormonal production moved exclusively into the overseers' realm.

When these drones began to moult, however, there were significant differences, complications which were unforeseen in the original circumstances. The process produced secretions within the drones which were toxic to the off-planet ruling castes. Furthermore, the moulting process did not always produce another viable Queen, but often some monstrosity that simply died outright, or else horrific warriors that took many with them in the process of their extermination.

It was certain that none of the mutations should be allowed to survive and risk propagation. The aberrant life-forms were too unreliable; beyond the randomness of their physical forms, their mentalities bore a recognizable trend towards deviance, and such alignment was a direct threat to the Hive.

And yet, though they be disposed as soon as the slightest hint of their transformations were recognized, the mutations were becoming more prevalent, more frequent and in increasing numbers, and so therefore had to be allowed to continue, undisturbed, for so long as it took for them to be studied and understood.

With understanding came the great conquering.

The monkey hammered an oblong rectangle, red, made of a material softer and less dense than the bludgeon. The overall effect was of the creation of a mess.

Richard was 'dreaming' again, in the chair with the myriad electrodes invading his body. Some tests they ran with the wireless codecs; this one they strapped him down for. It gave them the advantage of recording the sum-total kinesthetic experience, a stolen section of his life, that they could replay later and live for themselves. He didn't see why they should get so excited by it.

And yet, *this* poison-penned storyline was going to be one they weren't expecting. He'd discovered within himself the ability others called 'lucid dreaming', the art of consciously entering into the dreaming experience, and cooked up an idea he was eager to test out on his captors. He'd had no idea of how well it was going to work.

They'd taken him from his holding cell, injected him with strange chemicals, and led him to the focus-throne; his eyes sealed shut with a smear of spirit-gum, he was already falling asleep before they'd attached the last sensor below his groin and taped it in place. This time, instead of the welcome slide into oblivion, he narrowed in on the rise and fall of his breath and focused on the relaxing of his mind as his body altered its rhythms to the pulse of sleep. He was aware of becoming a string of light, of stretching to escape the confines of his physical form, of becoming energy captured in a knobby line that stretched from one end of the universe to the other. The blackness around him dissolved, and he stepped into another reality.

The monkey, a dream-representation of his basic animal nature, picked through the fragments of the red shape: there were gears, levers and bands, glowing spheres, sticky cubes, rods, cones and wands and all manner of jumbled components. This was going to be good, he thought. He'd even generate an image just for his captors, something to let them feel superior to him; with luck, it would distract them at just the right moment and buy him a few extra needed seconds.

The monkey picked its nose, contemplated the booger thoughtfully for a moment, and then put it in its mouth.

Then its hands went back down quickly to the pile of junk, sorting and arranging, categorizing and assessing, until it had just the right assortment of necessary parts.

And then the parts were forgotten again and put aside, but not left to disappear back into the void as so many other non-essential elements of dream often did. Instead, the monkey produced a typewriter for itself, something on which to hammer out some Shakespeare, and began methodically building the parts into the typewriter's body. Cones fit between cubes and spheres, attached by rods to bands of color which made up the insides of the machine; shapes merged with non-shapes on hinges of abstraction. It was left with a mutant thing, a device barely able to make the letters appear on a page between the clusters of attached detritus, a typewriter built by a committee of mythical Fae, something which never should have functioned but somehow did.

The monkey was pleased.

And Richard had not yet been forcibly resuscitated, which meant that the doctors had not yet fathomed what he was up to. He might just get away with it yet, and it was now or never. He had to work quickly.

The monkey's fingers danced over the keys.

"The quick brown fox jumped over the lazy dog, in breadth and width a fantastisk, singking, spheatly tchow of mightz."

In the fire-lit shadows of a fathomless cave, a dark Woman heard the monkey's call for help, and lent her power to its own.

Its voice washed against the words on the page, low and rough, a voice from the primordial ooze whose first call rang out over an untouched earth, and whose last cry would outlast all edifice of man. The unpronounceable letters battered against the page and tore through, ripped a hole clean through the paper and splattered wetly against the wall, dripping crimson trails of linguistic afterbirth down the walls of the monkey's cage. Another few words from the monkey's mouth, and it had burnt a hole clean through its confining walls.

Richard heard the shouting, smelled smoke, and smiled to himself. Without power running to the lab-equipment, his IV-drip would shortly stop and he'd soon enough have full control of his body. While he waited, he attempted to scan the minds of those around him. He still hadn't mastered that skill yet, though the panic and alarm going on around him was easy enough to discern without any special abilities. There would be destruction, and probably more than a few people would die. He didn't care. These were the people who held him prisoner, who opened his brain and peered inside to see how he worked, who tortured him to see what it would do. If breaking out of here meant that a few innocent people had to suffer, then it would be worth it. *Anything* would be worth it.

And there it was, the electro-mag cuffs fuzzing out and releasing him from the chair's clamping hold. This was his opportunity to escape.

This monkey was taking it to the streets.

From beneath deep waves of sleep-encrusted fog, Tom dredged himself up to the waking world, shaking his head and snorting out the night's congestion. He wondered where he was, it seemed like he *always* asked himself the question; it sure hadn't been the first time he'd asked it, nor would it be the last. The world's inconsistencies were a constant pressure, a grinding-wheel braced against his shoulders, bearing his down and tearing him to pieces. At the very least, he had a body of agony, a suit of meat and misery that remained constant, anchoring him to reality and guaranteeing that, even if he didn't have any clue *where* he was, he was sure it was *he* that was there, and it was he that would have to suffer again the next day, and the next.

He could always look forward to putting his foot down on the cold floor, whether that floor was carpeted or wood, concrete or tile; the nerves that recoiled in frozen shock would be his own. There was no way out.

He knew who it was that would stagger and crash until it found a place to relieve himself; he knew the feeling of cold water from the sink splashed on his face.

A face he didn't recognize, the stranger in the mirror a crawling mosaic of shifting features, splitting and running together like honey; a cloud of flies buzzed in through the bathroom window and swarmed around his head. Tom screamed and ran, arms flailing, from the room.

There were no flies, had never been any flies; he dropped his arms back down to his sides and searched the air for them; finding nothing, he crept cautiously back to the mirror to examine himself.

His face was gone. There really was nothing there, no ego to identify, no personality to the unrecognizable mess that kept changing before he could get a fix on it.

And now there were bells in his ears, somewhere high and to the right. Something was definitely wrong with him.

His heartbeat sped up, then slowed and thudded heavily in his chest; he felt as though he were breathing through a straw. If he couldn't pull himself together, he was sure he was about to pass out again. What could be going so wrong with him? What did he have? Was it all in his head?

Whose head was it?

He could still run; he could run out to the street and shout his confusion, could cry out for help.

He could see out through the fog, enough to find his way to the door.

Mongoose was at a loss.

He'd followed the outlander's trail as far as it was going to lead him, had almost gotten the prey into his hands, and then lost it at the last moment.

This wasn't like him, to not be able to fulfill his contracts. He kicked himself for his lapse in judgment; stopping to eat? What was he thinking? Was this some kind of deliberate self-sabotage? If his performance quotient didn't see a sharp rise, there might be values-recalibration training for him, and *that* was never anything to look forward to.

But then he caught an unexpected break.

His quarry was returning, arriving back at the same spot from which it'd departed. It looked like he was going to be able to fulfill his contract after all. The blinding beam of light rained down from above, leaving in its wake the thin, frail frame of his target. His hand went to his sidearm.

"MON2985, report!" It was more a whisper than a proper voice, a firm nudge inside his head, like a plucking of his tendons.

What the hell could it be now? His orders were clear; communications on this channel superseded any and all other priorities. Direct DomSec-linkages took precedence over all else.

He had to let the outlander go, for now. He gritted his teeth and formed the mental thrust of his reply.

"MON2985 reporting, orders?" The reply he got was astounding, and would vex him for the short remainder of his life.

The current base of operations was under attack, from some unknown vector within. He'd be apprised of events as they unfolded, but for now his presence was required back at HQ, as were all combat-ready units, self-preservation priority Beta. Intel was expecting a firefight.

He wondered if having a piece of silicon chip in his brain acting as a two-way radio was really a good idea, then shrugged it off alongside all his other job-related worries, and bent himself to the task at hand.

The outlander would have to wait for another time. It hurt him to have to leave his target behind, just when it was so close to his grasp; the sudden switching of priorities had never been one of his strong points.

Driving a normal land-based vehicle was probably the slowest conveyance he could have taken for his return aside from actually walking, but resources couldn't be spared for any of the more exotic means of transportation. He would probably arrive at the hot-zone just as it was cooling off.

This mission was turning into a botch on all accounts.

Cursing the outlander under his breath, he shifted into drive and tore off towards the freeway on-ramp at top speed.

HQ was a nightmare of disorder: people were milling about, black-clad guards rounding up the escaped subjects and other test-animals which had broken free of their confines, administrative staff being useless with clipboards and unrealistic demands. He was expected to retrieve their prime subject, a recorder from one of the wetware neuro-labs, who was the one responsible for all this chaos.

Surveying the scene, it was hard to believe that just one of the subjects could have been responsible for this much destruction. A single black plume of dense smoke billowed out from the reactor-labs to obscure the sun; the damage to that one facility alone would set back operations by at least six months. Something had set off a chain-reaction that ripped through the grounds, decimating their assets as a breathtaking pace. He'd arrived not long after the cleanup crew, but if they wanted to salvage anything of the facilities, they'd have to do better than they were currently. Maybe it was just a forfeit. He wasn't sure if it even could be recovered. Stepping over the charred remains of a severed hand, he ran the numbers and estimated the cost of rebuilding an underground fortress. It would be astronomical by the public's standards, one full year's worth of black-budget allotment.

He had no figures for human casualties; those were incidental. Human operatives were easily replaced.

A quick impulse from his cerebral-transceiver: he received the DNA-fingerprint for his quarry. Sniffing the air like a bloodhound, it was easy to tell that his target was no longer in the area. The scent was recent, but cold.

A moment later and the visual likeness of his intended target imprinted itself on his visual cortex. Too late, he realized; he'd already passed the man on his way in and dismissed him as one of the wandering invalids who were soon to be rounded up by the otherwise competent hospital-staff. He cursed once again, under his breath, for the second time that day, at a sense of timing gone wrong.

He doubled back; his target had vanished.

Richard staggered down the sidewalk; there was a fire behind him somewhere, and sirens, and he was wearing....a hospital gown?....for some reason, and he was unsure of where he was going. This was, or *should* have been, the easiest puzzle of them all to solve, the question of a destination, but he had to admit that it had him stumped. There was even a little urgency to it, he was pretty sure, but something was preventing him from focusing on the bigger picture.

He could handle the task at hand—the task at hand was putting one foot in front of the other, distancing himself from something back....there.

There were a million broken images fleeting past his mind's eye that attested to the nature of the 'something' which made it a thing to be avoided, of that he was sure; his mind blocked them out, though, and he wasn't sure just exactly what those images were, or what they had to do with anything. What the hell did fresh fish have to do with picking up his left foot, moving it forward, then picking up his right foot and moving it forward, where did fresh fish come in there?

He didn't know. He seemed not to care, if he checked. He wasn't sure how he felt about it, if at all. As if it mattered.

Right now was his time to run. He could have done other things: he could have succumbed to self-pity, and given up, laid down and waited for them to finish doing their thing with him; or he could have gotten lost in stupefaction, indulging the laziness of an idle, tunnel-visioned curiosity; or any of a number of petty distractions, but...

But there was an urgency in the need for movement, for putting a great distance between himself and something truly dreadful.

He remembered a building, a hospital without a waiting room and no other patients, or none that he was ever allowed to meet. Only him and all the doctors, prying with needles and electrodes, and steel-paneled walls. There were some invasions of his mind so penetrating they became rape, and he suspected the loss of his identity to be their doing.

The doctors had no names, only colors: doctor Green, doctor Blue, the dreaded doctor White. They all dressed and looked alike, a look he thought of as 'business-man grey'; the only colors they adopted were in their names alone, the doctors.

The doctors, in so far as he was concerned, meant trouble. He would run, and leave them behind with the chaos.

Tom had seen his chance, and taken it.

Tom; his name was Tom.

His name was Tom, and he was fleeing the hell he'd managed, this time, to remember.

There was something important about it, some overwhelming reason with which he was saddled, that made it his duty to bring it forward into memory. If only he could remember... There was just as powerful an impulse urging him to let it stay in the fog.

If he thought hard, he could recall an address that he could give to a cabdriver, though there wasn't any money in his pocket this time. It didn't matter. He now had a map home.

Catching taxis, even ones you didn't intend to pay for, was a lot easier if you were dressed in more than just a hospital-gown; he knew instinctively that there would be a house somewhere within a few miles of where he was, and that he shouldn't let himself be seen on his way there, but that he could make it by nightfall if he kept a steady pace. There was bound to be someplace he could break into, with a telephone and food and a change of clothing and an opportunity to lose the hunters.

Because he knew they would be after him as well, the hunters. Soon, they would be everywhere; the landscape would be crawling with them, inhuman beasts with his scent in their blood and their masters like the dark riders of the apocalypse. There was probably at least one already nearby, and those monsters wouldn't stop until he was either dead or back in captivity. The last thing he wanted was to return to the nightmare from which he'd just escaped. *Any* egress would do.

His luck was in: there was a house in the distance, a porch light on but otherwise dark, apparently empty and promising succor. It didn't take him long to reach it. The front door was unlocked, as if it were meant for him to shelter there. He let himself in and shut and locked the door. The quiet that dropped down around him was thick and painful with his thudding heartbeat. No one inside moved to prevent him from taking refuge there; he made his silent thanks to God (God? Who was that?) and prayed that nobody would appear to change the situation.

Ten minutes passed, another ten; he'd managed at last to get his panic under control—he wouldn't betray himself with a stupid move he could just as easily avoid by remaining level-headed and open to the obvious.

MON2985, it appeared, was to have a break in his streak of bad luck; his quarry had gone to ground close by. The runner was just an in-patient, no special training to speak of, which only made everything so much easier—the last thing MON2985 wanted to have to deal with was a firefight. He'd wasted too much time already going after the man, on top of losing his earlier subject. If things were to start going by the numbers again, who was he to argue?

The farmhouse loomed in the darkness. Tuning into the man's index, the hunter was able to see it through his target's eyes: how the porch light in the darkness had seemed a beacon of hope, the pain and the chaos behind him at his heels, the sure knowledge that nothing, not even this oasis of sanity in the night, would shelter him for long from the storm that followed on his heels. MON2985 would be only too happy to oblige. The man's terror tasted sweet on his tongue.

Was *this* really why he, Frank Constable, had joined up?

He approached the back door and read the man's signature inside, a shotgun pointed at the doorway, expecting him; for a moment, he considered the option of an upper-level insertion, a stealthy descent through the building and then finally capturing the target without him firing a shot or even suspecting that he'd been targeted, but...

Where was the fun in that?

And was it really right for him to take such pleasure in this?

The Mongoose hadn't been trained purely in stealth-ops; he'd also been schooled methodically in how to destroy his opponent psychologically. He could take the man down without a struggle but the target wouldn't learn anything from the experience. And he'd been briefed on the events surrounding the target's escape, as he'd arrived on the scene—one three-second blip on his transceiver told him the entire story of the man's subterfuge, how he'd deceived his kindly doctors, men who'd wanted nothing more than to help, with false promises of cooperation, accepting the lavish gifts and monetary payments they'd practically showered him with before suddenly and viciously turning on his generous providers and sadistically attacking them in his desperate escape. MON2985 understood there had been a hostage situation, that promises had been made and everything the man demanded had been provided, but the hostage had been killed anyway. He'd been shot in the back, a coward's murder.

A simple extraction was too good for a man like that. A man like that needed to be taught a lesson first, so that he would think twice before pulling any more stunts.

MON2985 came up to the back door and grabbed the handle, then stopped; he'd been working on instinct, not thinking it through to maximize the situation's potential. He let go, went back down to the bottom of the steps, and re-made his approach, being sure to scuff his feet and step heavily on the stairs.

Tom cowered against the strange refrigerator, the shotgun tucked into his shoulder; he'd found it in the den, as he knew he would, loaded and waiting for him. How he knew it would be there, nor how he knew it would also be supplied with shells, he couldn't say—he'd just assumed it would be there, exactly as he'd seen it in his imagination. It hugged up against his chest like an old friend.

In much the same way he knew where the gun would be, he became aware of his hunter's arrival. In his mind's eye, he saw the rather ordinary-looking man making his second approach to the back door, watched him turn the knob and push, saw the door in front of him in the real world slowly swing open with a creak, and held his breath as he waited for his pursuer to step around it and into his sights.

Tom's finger was already pulling back on the trigger as the door suddenly flew open and crashed into the wall. The ensuing muzzle-flash silhouetted the man's linebacker-framework against the darkness beyond, and Tom knew the man had to have caught the load square in the chest, but he continued forward into the room and barreled into him at full speed. Tom was knocked to the ground and the man landed on top of him, pinning him down and soaking his chest with something warm and wet that could only have been the stranger's blood.

There were lights appearing now, the bobbing beams of flashlights approaching through the yard, and by their dim glow Tom could see his attacker illuminated. The snarling creature atop him raised its fists and brought them pummeling down against his face, his nose, his ears; the man punched him in the throat and he coughed uncontrollably and struggled to get away but was pinned tightly beneath the larger man's weight, unable to shift it even slightly in his weakened state. He watched in horror as the man tore off a piece of his bloodied shirt and held the rag crumpled in his fist, which he pounded into his face again and again, and when the pain was almost too much to bear and he knew he was going to pass out, the man jammed the rag into his broken nose, exciting him with a sharp new pain that brought him quickly back to a total lucidity. The men with the flashlights, a team of SWAT-soldiers, had surrounded them and were watching his torture, and Tom could see clearly in the harsh glow of their torches that his shot had indeed caught the mad hunter square in the middle of his chest, a ragged wound defying explanation as to how he could still be alive, let alone bludgeoning him to a bloody pulp.

The man pulled the rag away from Tom's nose and held it over his face. "There. Your blood and mine. We are bonded, brother." He squeezed the rag, wringing out a stream of blood that dripped down into Tom's mouth. "Now I am within you forever. Wherever you run, there shall I be. Not even into death can you escape me, for I will find you even in the darkest of places. Forever, you are mine, motherfucker."

"Now, lights out," and he struck Tom one more time across the bridge of his nose, bringing on the total blackness of unconsciousness.

Chapter 3: ***Peabody's Amazing Engine***

Mister Peabody had been a sympathetic ear for Jeremy to unload his problems concerning Laylah; the man listened for hours while Jeremy wallowed in his self-loathing and misery, making little comment while he constantly blamed himself for her bad behavior. But then something had changed: the older man tried gently pointing out her fault, how the woman had brought him into her world without fully disclosing all her complications, and how she'd further abandoned him completely at the end without any kind of closure or even an explanation, but still Jeremy refused to listen to him. Finally Peabody had gotten angry at him and told him that if he refused to put the responsibility for the blame where it belonged, then he didn't want to waste any more of his time with it and Jeremy would be welcome to come back after he'd pulled his head out of his butt. Jeremy chose to stay away and sulk.

It took him several months to put himself together again enough to sort out his problems and face his friend. He'd gone through another round of finals and had a week before his next set of classes was supposed to begin, and was restless for something to do. He'd long ago given up cutting stamps for block-printing, and his painting had yet to come out from the long dead-end alley into which it had retreated, and something in his heart yearned painfully for stimulation. One evening, passing by the school's library, he remembered his last conversation with the professor, and though the burning sting of shame lit up his face, he determined to see the man again and rekindle their friendship. The mental gymnastics the man required of him kept him so entertained as to outdo any residual feelings of negativity that might have remained with him.

Jeremy sought him out on a Saturday afternoon, calling on the man in his own home, without first announcing himself. His old friend took him back into his confidences without question and the two were quickly back on track just like old times. Jeremy was so relieved to be again in the company of his fellow man that he followed rather more than led, letting the older man take the conversational reins. Peabody, soon exhausting his supply of new circumstances upon which to hinge his discourse, returned to where they'd last left off, before the unfortunate incident with the lady: the subject of 'weird science', and the Mesmeric-battery.

Their conversation drifted and meandered, ranging from subject to subject as their relations were explored; Peabody seemed to fixate upon scientists whose research concluded the existence of a luminiferous ether, a course of study that tended to be fatal amongst its proponents. And there were quite a large number of them, who Peabody covered in mind-numbing detail; Jeremy found his mind drifting as he pondered a number of different, more basic and wide-ranging, questions about the inadequacies of his education:

Why was he supposed to believe that Earthly humanity was the only intelligent life in the universe? Ever since he could remember, that had been the story—humans were the only game around, had always been and would always be so, the pinnacle of Creation. It had seemed like a world of such dimmed imagination and little possibility, but he went along with it. Everybody did. That was the way it went.

Why, if the body is an electrical phenomenon, are we taught it as a mechanical process? All the biology, anatomy and medicine he'd studied in school—what studying he'd actually done—had explained bodies as a collection of parts whose interactions were barely understood. He'd gone off-campus to look into Eastern medicine, and found a world of difference between the two schools wider than the oceans between them; the entire outlooks were from opposite perspectives. The conclusions he'd drawn from comparing the two led him to understand that he'd gone about it all wrong, that from day one he'd been looking at things backwards, that he'd been taught incorrectly how he worked, at a basic level. What exactly was disease, for that matter?

And why, for God's sake, had we all been taught to be slaves? And not just slaves, but the kind who kept the other slaves in line? There were anonymous-informant hotlines and morning work-whistles and neckties and ticker-tape mazes in front of the kiosks and alarm-clocks; there were cameras pointed at intersections and instructions printed on the box of toothpicks and designer labels for pet garments and parking meters on every stretch of downtown; there were campuses and work-release halfway-houses and courthouses with teller-windows and parking lots for churches with extra-long spaces. Everybody had their place, and you were expected to know yours and to work within its limitations; it was hardly ever said out loud, but it didn't need to be—it was almost unanimously reinforced. Why was he supposed to be what other people thought he was supposed to be?

Peabody wouldn't answer his first two questions, suggesting that they might be resolved if he were to check out the third answer for himself. Jeremy, still sensitive about their previous falling-out, took the man's terse answer as a rebuff, and excused himself for a recess, leaving with the excuse that he needed time to think over the information he'd been given.

"Yes, I would imagine so," was the only reply the professor made, and Jeremy was confused by what he perceived to be a mixture of regret, doubt and resignation in the man's expression. Jeremy took his leave in a hurry, fumbling with the knob and kicking the door-frame loudly on his way out, and forgot almost completely about him soon after.

The reason for the dismissal of his old friend was one totally commonplace: he met a girl.

Her name was Maria; she was a new transfer to the school, majoring in English with an eye for a teaching degree, and smart in a way that almost scared him. She was also, of course, a fiery beauty, with red hair that had natural white highlights, brilliantly hazel eyes, full pouting lips, a high forehead and the perfect hourglass figure. Whatever she'd seen in him was totally beyond his ability to guess, but they'd met by accident, found some common interest in an art exhibit, and soon struck up a fledgling romance.

In the course of their getting to know each other, Jeremy found himself recounting to her what he'd gone over with Lionel Peabody. They discussed the Mesmer-battery at great length, and even went so far as to recreate the device, or as close an approximation as they were able, based on the same underlying principles as the original creation. Here, Jeremy was to discover that its basic construction bore striking similarities to the devices of other, later, inventors, most especially the cancer-curing apparati of one doctor Wilhelm Reich, whose life-saving technology would invite his censure and even, some claimed, murder. Jeremy was credulous that anyone who could discover a cure for one of mankind's greatest ills would suffer such ostracism for it, but his new girlfriend gave him a knowing wink and poked him in the chest:

"Watch your back."

Agent MON2985 hung limply in the tank, immersed completely in the hydroxylene-jelly, dreaming the forced-reintegration of his body and mind in suspended animation. Memories drifted in and out through the uplink-wires attached to his head; concepts too large or complicated to efficiently transfer through his neural transponder-chip required the older hardware, with its wider bandwidth that was capable of transferring entire experiential memes in nano-seconds, enabling them to be chained in complete memory-sets; these engrams were recorded in the central data-banks, re-processed to suit the agency's agenda, and then uploaded back to the convalescent's memory-banks. It was technology 'stolen' from the outlanders, one they'd been encouraged to steal and coached in the art of its use. The humans had no idea of how they'd been cultivated in their self-enslavement.

While the jelly worked to restore his body, the machine-interface labored at the restructuring of his mind; where Frank Constable had been questioning his personal integrity in his participation with the great project, Agent MON2985 now felt great pride in his contribution to the betterment of humanity. Where once he'd harbored doubts as to the cagey morality of the overall design, he now saw clearly where compromises had been necessary and how sometimes what looked like a step backward was a very necessary stage in the overall growth-process. If he had once felt like the system was a giant boot stamping squarely on his head for the 'march of progress', he now understood that what he did was an obligatory step towards the perfection of history. The machine had such perspective, such visionary scope, that its ultimate clarity was impossible to deny. It was a total revelation, overwhelming and implacable, larger and more powerful than anything he could ever be.

First he saw the flashing lights; it always began with flashing lights, and a pure tone, and a gradual sliding agreeability as his brain compensated to match the external rhythm. Somatic memories began pulsing through his brain: the comfort and belonging of being at his father's side as he bagged a three-point buck, the cold sting of ice on his cheek falling while out skating with his first real girlfriend, the smell of homemade apple cider spiced with nutmeg on the day of his mother's funeral. The memories chained together, and interspersed between them came certain prepackaged concepts: love, duty, honor, trust. There were the usual fleeting images of party-members' faces, his commanders, the doctors to whom he reported, his missions-specialists and project-coordinators—the people to whom he was supposed to dedicate his life and service—and they were again associated with the core duty-concepts.

Obedience.

Allegiance.

Acceptance.

Obey.

Faith.

Believe.

Obey.

Obey.

The lights flashed against his closed eyelids, timing their rhythm against his shrinking irises and letting him know just exactly how he was supposed to feel. Whenever there was some question of association, or if the subject-matter had a tendency to confusion or mixed priorities, his orientation could be fixed squarely with the proper stimulation of the appropriate glandular-clusters, creating whatever series of hormonal secretions the machine's algorithms deduced to trigger the desired response. Agent MON2985's reactions had been decided and preprogrammed for him, before he ever knew what he'd be responding *to.*

He was becoming sure, *quite* sure, that his involvement in the project was right, and it was just.

The project was necessary, and he was valued.

Tom opened his eyes: it was probably mid-afternoon, a weekday. The house he was in looked familiar, and he recognized the woman bringing him a cup of coffee as someone who'd been nice to him in the past.

"Are you feeling better, sugar? I was worried about you. You've had a fever of a hundred and four for the past two days. I don't know why I let you stop me from taking you to the hospital."

"No hospitals, I'm fine." He wasn't sure where the words were coming from.

"If you're not any better by tonight, then no deal, mister. I'm not gonna lose you. Here, let me take your temperature." She held a glass thermometer in her hand, expectantly. Tom opened his mouth without offering any resistance.

"Well, it's down to a hundred and one, but you're not out of the woods yet. I'm going to keep you in bed for at least another day."

"And how do you expect to keep me in bed, woman? Eh?" He patted the empty space next to him with what appeared to be a playful lecherousness, but the act wasn't fooling him. He didn't know who she was, what he was doing there, or why he felt anything for the woman at all. He didn't really mean the invitation, he was just doing it because he thought it was the right thing to do.

"Ohh, you. No, you're in no place to be wearing yourself out like that... But just you lay back, and I'll see if I can't help you get at least a little better."

He was possessed, for the briefest of interludes, of a passing uncertainty, a questioning of the basic validity of the situation in which he found himself; the sudden warmth between his thighs and the pleasure were enough to remove all doubt from his mind.

After, he insisted on smoking a cigarette in spite of her protestations (and what was her *name*, anyway? Why didn't he know?) and the harshness of the smoke on his fever-choked lungs. He thought it was something he liked to do. He couldn't understand why.

Richard regained consciousness in the cold embrace of the machine's emanations.

He had been dreaming, and his thoughts and everything they'd encapsulated had been recorded. No telling now if they had discovered the mechanism whereby he'd hidden his intentions from them before; that may have become an option no longer available to him.

The potential loss of his last vestige of privacy came as a devastating blow to him. They'd taken everything from him, starting with his freedom and his trust in his fellow man, then on to his individuality and his sense of purpose, and now finally to his very being. There was no part of himself that he fully owned, nothing of himself that was exclusively his—he belonged to them, in body and soul.

For just a little while, he'd dreamed of escape, had held the fragile idea in his hands and forged it into a weapon, which he'd wielded with a terrible ferocity against his captors....but even that had been useless.

And now that he was thinking about it and remembering, he could sense their computers stacking up his memories, tearing them down into their essential components and rebuilding them, formulating defenses against every move he'd made, becoming stronger and less susceptible to tactics which were even remotely similar to what he'd accomplished. He'd never be able to try it again, or anything like it, without his moves being anticipated by their damnable machines and countered.

The IV began his nutrient-drip; there was more than the usual amount of morphine in it, today. He was sure he'd be totally addicted and helpless by the time they let him come fully out of his coma. He hated them, *hated* them, for it.

The machine was to him both mother and destroyer.

Jeremy spent the end of his summer getting lost in Maria. She was a good medicine for him, and he gradually came the long way back from where he'd fallen. She got him to start going out more, taking him on gallery walks, tours of the city's coffee-shops, and even to the occasional party, though he still wasn't quite ready to take on the nightclubs, with their public displays of rowdy living and human sweat.

One day she took him by surprise: "Can I talk to you about something intensely personal?"

"Sure." He wasn't sure, but for her he was willing to take the risk. She had been becoming increasingly close to his center, and had a way of finding out his hidden faces that made him both uncomfortable and elated. She was worth whatever emotional risks she demanded he take.

"Okay, then, here it is. Now, I've noticed this thing that happens with you sometimes, when you're talking to other people, it's like they lose interest halfway through whatever you're saying and then start fidgeting or being distracting or they start talking to someone else or whatever... Please don't take this the wrong way—oh, I can see I've already hurt your feelings."

Jeremy was quick on the uptake. "No, no it's alright. It's just that I know what you're talking about. It drives me crazy. What can I do about it?" A quick stab of fear jabbed him in the chest: was this the set-up? Had she seen the real him, and this was how she began the 'Look, you're a really great *friend...*' speech?

"Look," she said, "you're a really great friend...."

Jeremy had time to wonder, for just a moment, if she'd actually heard his heart land by his feet. They always did this to him. Next thing you knew, they'd be holding the bloody knife.

She went on, "...and I can't stand seeing this happening to you. I know exactly how it feels. It used to happen to me, too."

"What, you? Really?" Jeremy's words collided. This was not something that ever happened to him; this wasn't the way the world usually worked.

"Yeah, me. And I remember it hurt. A lot. *When* I let myself notice how I felt about it. Most of the time I was in a kind of denial, I guess. Either I tried to ignore it or I blamed it on everyone else."

"So, what'd you do about it?" At this point he was talking on autopilot.

"I had to discover for myself how to keep people's attention, but first I had to figure out whether or not I really *wanted* it. Half the time that was my problem. I was trying to impress people I didn't really like, so I was inadvertently sabotaging myself. Also, I had to really believe that I was worth listening to. *That* was a fun one to work out, lemme tell you. Sarcasm alert."

"Yeah, I got that. Wow, I really appreciate your honesty with me. It seems like everyone else I know is so fake, what's your angle, huh?"

"No angle, Jeremy. I just like you."

He kissed her then, for the first time, and then took her out for ice cream. It was the best ice cream he was ever to have in his life.

Several days later he brought her to meet Mister Peabody. The older man was happy to see his young friend yet again, and was understanding of his absence upon meeting Maria. He met them on the steps, holding the door open and beckoning Maria to enter. She looked down at his round, white head and laughed lightly, thanking him and making her way inside. The professor followed her with his droopy eyes for a second and then turned to Jeremy:

"Oh, she's lovely. Good job, my boy. Now do come inside."

"Thanks." Jeremy felt a stab of jealousy, quickly dismissed it and went inside.

Maria wandered through the man's house, a claustrophobic maze of antique scientific instruments and gadgets, piled high to the ceiling in boxes and on shelves. She and Mister Peabody talked and became acquainted, each taking quickly to the other, leaving Jeremy to stew in an imagined exclusion. To his credit, Peabody chose that moment not to take offense at Jeremy's childish behavior, instead opting to engage both of them in conversation:

"So, Jeremy, have you told your new friend about any of our earlier discussions?"

Maria answered for him, while Jeremy sulked by the wall. "Oh, you mean about, like, alternative medicine and that stuff?"

"Yes, that stuff," Peabody replied, "Well, good. I'm glad Jeremy has found a partner who shares such common interests. Oh, dear, I hope I haven't been overly presumptuous..."

"Well, no, not entirely. I think he's starting to grow on me, even if he is being a pill right now. Come on, Jeremy, join the conversation. Please?"

Jeremy was reluctant to let go of his resentment. "Ehh, I'm

not 'being a pill', I just don't feel like talking right now."

"It's alright, no one will try to force you. Perhaps, Maria, I could change the subject—I have something I'd like to show you. Tell me what you think of this...." The professor disappeared into the depths of his house; they heard him rummaging about in the back and he returned a moment later with a sparkling lump held out in his hand, which he offered to the girl. "There, what do you make of it?"

She took the strange object from him and turned it over, inspecting it carefully: it appeared to be made of some kind of plastic, with bits of metal suspended in it. "I don't know. What is it?"

Peabody cleared his throat. "What you have there is a block of a substance I'm calling urgomite."

"Urgomite? What the heck is that?"

"Yeah, what is it?"

"Oh, good, Jeremy. I'm glad I could at last spark your interest. Well, you remember the last we spoke about the inventions of Doctor Reich, yes? This is a modern extension of some of his ideas pertaining to the purposeful direction of the flow of etheric plasmas."

"Whoa, you just said a mouthful, doctor P. How about clearing that up a little bit, for those of us without the pointy hats with stars on them?"

"I like your sense of humor, girl. Alright, then. Its construction is simple, a handful of thinly sliced metal shards mixed into a solidified parcel of fiberglass resin, with a humble quartz crystal embedded in its middle. The basic materials are in direct correlation to the apparatus of doctor Reich, the orgone accumulator—orgone being the name given to the electric fluid he discovered motivating all life—whereby he could concentrate such energies with a layered arrangement of metals and plastics, much like you would find here, the main difference being that the doctor's devices were built of orderly, patterned layers of the two substances and were missing entirely the quartz element. The crystal, when once compressed by the shrinking action of the polymer as it hardened, throws off a piezoelectric charge which further excites the material's natural energy-gathering qualities. That's the theory behind it, at any rate."

"In one ear and out the other, but I think I got the general gist. Well, Mister Wizard, I gotta say that while I might not understand it completely, it sure is pretty."

"And I'm certainly glad you think it so, Maria. Go on, I'd like you to have it."

"What? No, I couldn't take this away from you...."

"There, there—I can make as much of it as I like. Please, do take that home with you. I insist."

"Well, I have to give you something for it."

"It is my gift to you. If you feel duty-bound to return something for it, you could report back to me any interesting findings you may discover in its presence—I would certainly take that as adequate compensation."

"Gee, thanks mister," said Maria, and put the sparkling lump into her pocket.

Later, when they'd returned to Jeremy's apartment, Maria took the block of plastic out of her pocket and held it up to catch the light, gazing at herself in the reflections off the metal shavings within.

Jeremy broke her spell of concentration. "You guys sure seemed to hit it off. You think there's anything to it?"

Her eyes focused and she came back from whatever inner vision she had been witnessing. "I don't know, you tell me. He's your friend."

There was just barely the hint of defensiveness to Jeremy's tone of voice. "Yeah, maybe, but this was the first time I'd actually seen him bring out any of his stuff. He's never shown me anything like that before. I wonder if it really works like he says."

"Oh Jeremy, what am I going to do with you?"

"I don't know. What do you want to do with me?"

She dropped the lump of urgomite beside him on the bed and sat down next to him. "You really shouldn't have to ask."

She made love to him that night, for the first and only time.

In their passion, neither of them noticed who had knocked the block of metal and plastic to the floor, where it rolled under the bed and lodged itself in shadow, nor would they likely have cared.

Still later that night, after Maria had said her goodbyes and left, Jeremy had trouble getting to bed—no matter what position he took, he found himself increasingly uncomfortable and unable to lie still long enough and relax to the point where he would be able to fall asleep.

When at last he did manage to nod off, his dreams were continuously interrupted with a barrage of intense imagery and fraught with nightmares. In most, he was pursued by an unkillable monster of giant proportions intent upon his destruction; in the worst of them, he was the perpetrator.

He dreamt of a high hill: there was a path, bordered by arching poplars that canopied overhead and blocked out all the light of the full moon above. There was no noise, no insects humming, but for the tread of feet on hard earth.

He was young, perhaps seven or eight, naked and carrying a large ornate knife; his parents were on either side of him on the path, and they were egging him on with promises of rewards waiting for him at the top of the hill. Jeremy, his tiny body shivering with cold, snarled at them and waved the knife behind him at his father; a breeze pulled the branches aside for a moment and moonlight illuminated a row of evil runes along the blade and caught in a brilliant ruby mounted near the handle. His father's eyes widened in surprise at finding his son threatening him with the blade and he slapped the boy across the face.

"Save it for the ritual, boy," his father hissed at him, and shoved him along the path towards its end. In the distance, he made out the flickering of a bonfire in the middle of a clearing; he could tell they were near the end of the trail. "Almost there. You gettin'...?" and then his father's words devolved into backmasked mumble. The wind howled in protest at such blasphemy.

His mother was quick to respond. "You know he's still too

young, yet. Why do you keep trying to push him?"

Father was less than sympathetic. The words he spat at her over his head felt like poison to Jeremy and came out as gibberish, an alien tongue mouthing an unspeakable language.

And then the words came clearly, "I won't have him growing up soft on me."

His mother said something by way of reply but it was lost in the rushing gale of the cyclone above them; the dream shifted and Jeremy found himself on his knees in the center of the clearing, sometime later, blood dripping off the knife and running down his upraised arm, his side blistering from the heat of the bonfire, a young girl peppered with stab-wounds lying at his feet. He lowered the knife and looked stupidly at his hands. Surrounded by people in animal-masks and bizarre costumes, he alone was without a stitch of clothing, his nakedness covered only by the gore brought up from the girl before him.

Choking with shame, he felt the urge to vomit overtaking him and he rose to his feet; a fox in the audience asked him: "What are you doing?" and put her hand on his shoulder. He pushed her away but she insisted on coming back to him. The heat was becoming too intense to stay where he was any longer and he tried to shove his way through the crowd of onlookers, but they caught him and put him back into the circle with the fire.

The fox persisted in grabbing at him, taking his arm with the interrogative "Where are you going?" He knocked her arm away and pulled off her mask.

"What's wrong with you?" a younger Laylah asked him.

Jeremy spent the next two days incapacitated with the worst migraine he'd ever experienced in his life; everything else was put aside as he tackled the enormity of dealing with such mundane tasks as tying his shoes, or brushing his teeth, or lifting his eyelids, with the handicap of a three-hundred-pound gorilla on his back driving tent-pegs into the sides of his skull. Maria came to visit him, briefly, but didn't stay for long;

Jeremy, in the grip of infirmity, was loose with his language and mercilessly harangued the poor girl with his misery. She did her best to offer him some comfort, made him a cup of herbal remedy tea, and then left him to cope by himself.

For two days, Jeremy shivered and shook, sweating profusely at the least exertion, overtaken by the powerful constriction in his temples. On the break of the third day, he awoke from a dreamless sleep to find the pain blissfully gone away and, battered and drained, picked himself up to resume his life.

He tried to get Maria on the telephone but she wasn't picking up; Jeremy suspected that she was avoiding him.

When three more days had passed and he was still unable to get through to her, he began to suspect she might be dumping him; his calls went unreturned, she didn't come to her door when he came knocking, she was never at any of her usual hangout-spots. If he'd been less self-absorbed, he might have wondered if there were maybe something wrong, perhaps something serious, that had occasioned her absence, but Jeremy was not yet at that point of his personal growth and the idea never occurred to him. Instead of getting worried, he got glum and resentful, suspecting her of treachery. His answer was to drink.

On the evening of the sixth day after Jeremy had seen Maria for the last time, he had another nightmare, far worse than the one that signaled the onset of his headache.

He dreamt of the path again, and the clearing at the top of the hill; there was another bonfire lit, the flames whipped violently by furious winds that threatened destruction.

There was a strange man there, someone he'd never seen before, leading the group. He wore a suit under his robe.

When the man demanded Jeremy get down on his knees and fellate him, his father pushed him to the ground. When he resisted, his father took the bloody knife away from Jeremy and cut him on the hand.

...On the back of his hand, where he'd have a scar...

A throaty female voice next to him croaked, "Good, good!"

and he looked over at its source and into Laylah's hungry eyes.

It was his birthday. Why did it have to happen on his birthday?

His father loomed over him against the blackened sky, a monster in the night wearing elk-antlers.

"I got her ready for you now, boy. Time for you to become a man. About fuckin' time, too. You make me sick."

His mother said something he couldn't understand, commanding him to do something to which he'd never admit.

Jeremy did as he was told, and something became different.

He woke up, shaking, and ran to the bathroom to vomit. Laylah was waiting for him there, lying in the bathtub, covered to her waist in blood.

"Oh my God...," Jeremy stuttered as she smiled at him, her mouth blistering and dripping a black, oily sludge, and lifted her pelvis. Her labia parted, and it spoke to him:

"No, not your God. You know not who that is."

It spat at him, smudging his cheek with blood. Jeremy screamed and backed away, wiping at his face.

"Our God stinks of the pit, boy. Come away with me to destruction."

Jeremy screamed again and tripped, falling over backwards, and landed on the fire.

He woke a second time, shouting himself into the new day. After a few moments, his heart slowed its triphammering and settled into a more normal rhythm, and before another few minutes had passed, the dream had receded into the blackness of Lethean fugue. Jeremy began his day with shaking hands and hot-flashes, preparing for a bout with the flu.

Beneath his bed, forgotten and unassuming, a block of shimmering plastic that had rolled behind an old shoe-box released a vaporous cloud of white plasma, which then vanished as soon as it had appeared. Jeremy never noticed it, and the block of urgomite lay softly humming to itself for a while, and then quieted.

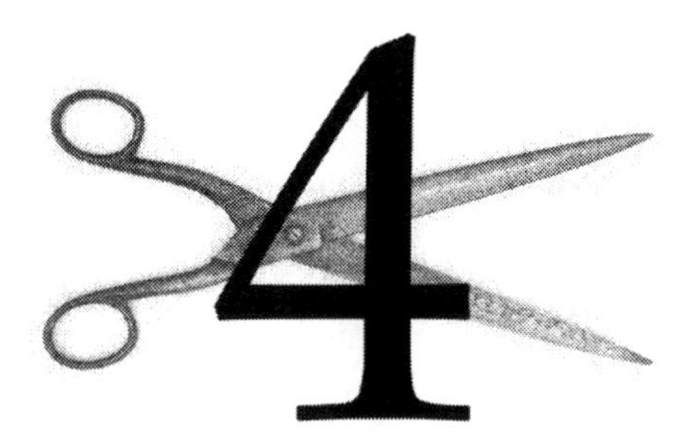

Chapter 4: ***The BEAST You Know***

MON2985 had a splitting headache; he always did when the head-fucker machines got through with him. This time he was a little fuzzy on just what 'adjustments' had been done to him, but he could tell they must have been fairly substantial values-alterations for him to feel as disoriented as he did. When he looked at the calendar and saw that he'd lost *two whole days*, he knew the adjustments had to have been more drastic than he'd first thought.

The Party brooked no deviation; he was proud to be kept in line. He opened the door, hung the 'Do Not Disturb'-sign on the knob, closed the door. There had been no one in the hall.

He'd received two new sets of orders, from different branches: DomSec needed him to program and implement an interrupt for an UC4—that would be a type 4 urbane citizen, an inactive sleeper-agent, typically low-priority—and the skyboys still wanted him to run interference on the outlander he'd lost previously. The orders were not to conflict and it was assumed he could and would run both concurrently. He didn't understand why he'd been given the UC4, those types were usually handled by the more mundane spooks in the NSA, or even the CIA-clowns; that it should be handed down to him came as a mystery.

But not a mystery he'd bother trying to understand. His was not to question why; his was but to do, or die.

This hotel was better than most he'd occupied; this one had supplied him with a desk and chair. He muttered darkly to himself as he plugged the adapter into the wall-socket and attached the cord to the back of his laptop.

The cranial uplink in his head was an excellent means of receiving communications from Central but for what he was supposed to do he'd need a hardwired terminal; he kept a laptop computer for such tasks. It neither required any special software nor stored any sensitive data on its drive, and so was 'safe' for him to leave unattended in storage while he was away; logging in to the 'BEAST'-network was secured via a system of chained relays that interacted both with the laptop and the transceiver-chip in his skull, as well as a live SysOp attached to the mainframe server for real-time judgment calls.

MON2985 called up the terminal-prompt and logged in to the network. His assignment parameters popped up for him and he reviewed the case: 24 year old Caucasian male, unmarried, no dependents, negligible extended support-network... The details were relatively commonplace and uninteresting. Evidently this one had a filial web who raised him in a typical Deist anti-cult, of a type that MON2985 had cut his teeth instigating and promoting when he was new in the Agency. He'd always found the Satanist enclaves brutish and lowbrow but they were fiendishly effective at establishing a solid trauma-base for the Monarch-assets, especially if they were introduced as children—the younger the better—by their primary care-givers. It was a technique the Agency had borrowed, actually, sometime in the early days when it was still a fledgling outfit, from forgotten operatives who'd been at it already for a long, long time. Frank hadn't trusted any of the non-local attaches with whom he'd interacted, but he'd always followed his orders.

Always followed his orders.

His orders.

Orders.

Or—

There was a problem with the interrupt he'd been ordered

to run; something was malfunctioning with the radionic index, either the lock wasn't taking or else the signal had run into some kind of bizarre quantum feedback-loop. It wasn't unknown to happen, but almost never with an UC4, and definitely not with one who'd taken his kind of anti-cult conditioning—their minds weren't equipped to shake off the hostile signals. For curiosity's sake, he pulled up the subject's profile. A closer look at 'J. M. Proctor (USA) 2278' might give him some insight as to how he'd slipped the index.

The Agency's computer-system was an octopus, its tentacles wrapping the world; there was no spot on Earth outside its reach. All known facts about a person's identity, anything that distinguished them as an individual, went into their file. Any time they were late for work; decided to skip lunch; cheated on their wives or husbands; fought with their neighbors or ran for office; an entry corresponding their motives, actions and outcomes went down on their permanent record. From the time you were born 'til such time as you died, the machine had your number.

All citizens had a small sample of their genetic material collected from them, usually at birth; the unique signatory aspects—DNA sequences were one such example—were decoded and archived in the BEAST's central data-banks. The human psyche had long since been analyzed and codified, and the BEAST had an entire library of complex programs and subroutines it was capable of running against any individual, group or subset of the population that its programmers had targeted. The BEAST computer was capable of remotely accessing almost any and every single human being on the planet.

The original machine had been born in a secret location somewhere in eastern Europe, a giant hive of mainframes that had grown over the years and taken on girth of city-proportions. Riding piggy-backed along the lines of humanity's social and industrial evolution, it grew its body piecemeal around the world as the technology came into the hands of differing nations. Some claimed that the network had spontaneously generated artificial intelligence all on its own; others, that it had become infested with disembodied outlander-entities, or by demons from another dimension; still others theorized that the machine's unpredictable actions were not actual intelligence, but the results of virus-code inserted by the aliens. Agent MON2985 was not one who speculated.

It was known to occasionally initiate programs of its own against unknown subjects for its own inscrutable purposes, and this was why a human SysOp was always online, in case such programs were deemed counter-productive to the Agency's goals.

It appeared, in this case, that J. M. Proctor's immunity had nothing to do with the BEAST's intervention—the computer was known to let the random urbane off the proverbial hook—nor did it appear to correspond to any other of the handful of incidental events that always seemed to go in unison with this type of situation. There had been no major behavioral-changes listed in his history: no life-threatening injuries, no major or even minor chemical dependencies begun or ended, no startling alterations to the subject's ideologies. Nothing. A near-death experience or even an extreme change of religion could be enough to alter a person's holographic-imprint, but this person had no event in his recorded history to account for such a change.

There was a recent interpersonal-relationship, with romantic overtones. It didn't rate much on the significance scale according to the BEAST's calculations, but it might merit some attention. If he was unable to get to the subject directly through his index, he'd start the interrupt through the subject's immediate support-network.

He took a brief pause, after the keystrokes which initiated the little currents of fate that altered people's lives had tapped their song of doom onto the airwaves, and questioned the validity of his actions. He was breaking up a college-kid and his girlfriend. Was *this* really what the Agency was about? Was he to serve no more petty a function than to increase the sum total of misery in the world?

Tiny beads of sweat appeared across his brow; he pushed the laptop away in frustration and rubbed his eyes.

Was it *right*, what he was doing?

And then there was a short, stabbing pain in his head, and the questions faded away into nothingness.

He knew who he was, and what he wanted.

He wanted to do his job.

He'd been processing the interrupt for a couple hours, pouring over the details of the subject's life and of those close to him, still unable to determine why none of the usual triggers were effective in his case. MON2985 hadn't been authorized to access Proctor's sleeper alpha-programming, in which case he could ply his option of keys upon him in a brute-force attack to crack open the subject's conditioned-reflex engrams and see which would take; as it was, he'd all but exhausted the tier-one information on the kid. If he thought the name and occupation of the guy's third-grade teacher would be of some benefit to him, then he could start plumbing the tier-two data or even further, but there would be no end to it and no use in doing so, that he could see. The subject was eluding him. This was becoming too much of a habit.

His method wasn't working; perhaps another approach...

The interrupt had been ordered approximately a day and a half ago, when he was in the tank for 'readjustment therapy', and had been discovered to be problematic almost immediately, glitchy and unresponsive. A quick scan of the immediate history surrounding the order showed nothing unusual: the subject performed his normal daily routine and had minor contact with his romantic interest—again, nothing significant.

The hair on his forearms prickled; was there someone behind him? He actually moved first, physically turning his head to look, before remembering to use his psi-scan. There was no one, but his cheeks stung just the same.

A close look at the e-docket showed the label "USAF—DSD/INT"; Deep-Space Division, Intelligence. The skyboys.

This meant one thing, and one thing only. Occasionally,

mysterious orders were handed down the chain of command from a dark arm of the Agency, a deep department so black as to be completely opaque, even from the inside. There was no rumor to be had as to its origin or purpose—no such thing as the rumor mill at his level of operation, loose lips were soon sealed—but he'd been assigned emissary once and gained the hard-earned knowledge that deep-space int meant that commands were issued by the outlanders, whether for their own internal policing or for treaty-enforcement, or...

There—there it was again. *Was* there someone behind him?

His head started to ache—it was an area best left alone.

But to understand the situation and how he was to carry out his orders, his *very specific* orders, he had to put everything in context. Orders pertaining to alien issues required an alien understanding.

These kinds of mental gymnastics allowed him the room to think the unthinkable.

No one knew exactly when the outlanders had first arrived on Earth; there had been archaeological and anecdotal evidence of their presence here since the beginning of time, so far as anyone could determine. It also appeared that they'd been instrumental in guiding human evolution in a very physical sense, from Neanderthal man to Cro-magnon, and then to have steered events in our development through the ages, from the establishment of royal dynasties to the discovery of new technologies and religions. There was some speculation as to whether the outlanders suppressed humankind's advances more than they encouraged them, but these speculations never lasted for long...

They'd agreed to treaties in the early nineteen-fifties and signed documents with representatives of the Earth's larger governing bodies; they were to give us free access to certain of their devices, which would be handed over to the research scientists and engineers who'd take them apart and puzzle over their secrets, and the outlanders were to be allowed to harvest humans for genetic materials. There'd been infractions upon the terms of the treaties, immediately, on both sides. The outlanders took many times more than the number of people they'd been allowed, few of whom were actually returned unmodified; it'd become a damage-control nightmare, the need to suppress the truth of the situation from leaking into public knowledge.

And Earth pilots had almost immediately resorted to attacking outlander craft in hopes of finding new gadgets to reverse-engineer. It was amazing how infrequently such discoveries were made, how elusive the greys' ships could be, how freakishly clean of all but the bare necessities the alien craft were. Agency craft were always better-equipped, had been since the beginning, even before the first outlander vessel was shot down over the New Mexico desert. Agency anti-gravitic vehicles, developed in the chaos immediately following the second World War by immigrant Nazis, were primitive by comparison and incapable yet of interstellar travel, but they made up for a lack of power with an excess of *style*. At least you could get a decent drink on board a good old-fashioned Earth-saucer.

The Agency itself had been formed around a core group composed mainly of repatriated Nazis, imported to the US at the end of the war, who brought with them their research into electro-magnetic wave propagation and related propulsion systems. Such knowledge was at the deep-black level of national security for obvious reasons, including the security of the oil-based energy-economy, and concordant measures were taken to keep the program secret. It was a snowballing kind of secrecy, grown increasingly massive with each passing decade, until the Agency had become the monolith it was today.

A monolith whose full brunt had come to bear upon the back of a college kid and his girlfriend, to break them apart, because an alien wanted it so.

It didn't seem right.

Another short, stabbing pain convinced him otherwise.

He seemed to be in the mood for breaking rules; he decided a little unauthorized, machine-assisted remote-viewing could be in order. The psi-talent was normally only allowable under requisition, and under the careful guidance of a skilled monitor; since he often subbed as monitor for others, he justified the breach in protocol to himself as excusable.

His sliding-scale priorities were going to get him into trouble one day, if he wasn't careful.

There was a headset-unit which looked like nothing more out of the ordinary than a pair of stereo-headphones; he donned the gear, connected the plug to his laptop, and launched the software that opened his mind to the fullness of the universe.

He could say this about the R.V.-procedure: if it had ever happened, anywhere in the multiverse, it could be witnessed. This was not necessarily a good thing. Even with limiters in place keeping the subjective events to those within the realm of current possibility, there was still the danger of becoming lost in the vast realm of the plausible. It was too easy for a remote viewer to wander into proscripted realms and mess with the causality-index—and that was the ultimate 'catch' involved: any remote viewing inevitably involved some kind of remote *influencing*, due to the presence of the observer. Many timelines could be expected to snap back to their predestined causality-indexing without any undue skewing of the mainline (at least it was thought so by the Agency theorists, it was still an undeveloped school of thought and largely untested) but the Protocols had been put into practice to prevent testing the limits of reality's compensatory twistings. It was *not* an issue many were willing to press.

Agent MON2985 leaned back into his chair and allowed the emanations from the 'phones to recalibrate his brainwaves. It was different for everyone; for him, it always started with the tunnel of colored lights. A few minutes to let himself adjust and then he was adrift in the data-flow. He tried to hone in on the subject Proctor 2278 but the only visuals he got were darkness and a slippered foot before his visual range broke down into fields of unpatterned static. Auditory was no help either: a ringing telephone was answered with a "Hello?" before that signal, too, degraded into noise. MON2985 attached himself to the subject at any number of his predictable nodes: waking routine, food routines, sleep and recreation routines—the subject remained unreadable. As soon as he'd managed to lock onto something about the man, some kind of randomized spread-frequency cross-modulation would knock him offline. After the seventh time rebooting his laptop he began to get frustrated and angry. If he couldn't get to Proctor by the direct route, he'd find another vector.

There was an old romantic interest from his past; with the interrupt sub-routines already working on the current RomInt, bringing the old one back into the picture could cause some amusing drama. Besides, the old RomInt was an UC1, an active collaborator, and he would be able to bi-locate through her nervous system and get a direct line-of-sight on the primary target. Fuckin' kid. He'd pay before this was through.

A few more keystrokes, and Fate once again was altered at the whim of a man.

A voice cut in through his headset: "This is an unauthorized transactional process. Cease and desist, MON2985, that is an order."

Oh, hell. So he'd been monitored after all, and he'd let his emotion get the better of his judgment. While they were watching. He knew it didn't look good.

"Don't worry, I'm not going to report it. I'm not even going to cancel the sub-routine. You do good work, MON2985. Generally speaking."

He let his breath out slowly, suddenly unsure of where this interaction was going. He'd been caught using unauthorized psychotronics, which carried a stiff penalty—now it looked as if he wasn't to be censured at all. What gave?"

"Just don't let it go to your head. You're to re-prioritize the outlander and pursue that now. Disconnect from this network and power down your machine. That is all."

Arrogant bastard. So he was to go after the outlander now, eh? Fine, just as well. He'd had enough techno-frustration for one day and needed the change of pace. Besides, he was confident he'd succeed in tracking down and capturing it, and he could definitely use a win to show off about now. His missions were becoming a string of failures. His standing in the Agency was suffering; at this point in his life, the Agency was all he had left. Without it, he would surely fall apart.

HfX7qe2179A9 had deliberately disobeyed a royal summons.

Twelve entire earth-rotations had passed since it first received the summons, and it had chosen not to answer. Instead, it kept busy, refusing to allow itself to dwell upon the Queen, as if doing so would prevent Her from remembering and reaccessing it; this did nothing to stop the Queen's quiet, incessant urging in its head. Furthermore, time spent away from the pod meant that its equipment would go uncharged and begin to break down; it had already been forced to shuff off the protective suit when it started becoming too brittle to flex. It did not know how long it could keep up; a fugitive on an unknown world, HfX7qe2179A9 could go anywhere it wanted, but nowhere would be home.

On the fourth day of its exile, it tried tracking down the human it had spared—surely the boy would help it.

HfX7qe2179A9 chose at first not to use the wand to silence the boy; its newfound appreciation for sovereignty and self-awareness would not allow it to rob another of the same...

But the boy had screamed, and called for help, and it had used the wand after all. Just a little.

The rest of the human's family was put to sleep, the boy made docile and induced to view it as something familiar to him, as someone the boy trusted, and HfX7qe2179A9 tried to engage the boy on an emotional level.

Emotions were entirely new and complex to HfX7qe2179A9; the boy had been its first exposure to 'feeling', and was the one with whom it wanted to demonstrate and explore the experience.

The human turned out not to be cooperative.

HfX7qe2179A9 planted the idea in his mind of trust, cooperation, mutual benefit and reward, then allowed the boy to regain his pure attention; HfX7qe2179A9 knew that a shared feeling had to be the real thing, unaltered.

The boy screamed again. HfX7qe2179A9 hadn't allowed the parents to return to consciousness, so no one interrupted them, but the boy's refusal of it had been unpleasant.

Hurt. Another new experience. It grew vexed.

Whipped in the gale of novel emotions, HfX7qe2179A9 reached out to the boy—to stop him, to pull him close, to push him away—it didn't know what it would do or why. Movements that followed their own reasons were also unknown to it. All it knew was that it wanted the boy, and the boy did not want it, but still it reached.

The boy screamed again and struck out, and HfX7qe2179A9's arm broke off at the elbow and came away in the child's grasp, who went hysterical. Streams of liquid sprang from his eyes and nose and his wailing reached a new fevered pitch; he called for his mother and his father, and he screamed the awful words at HfX7qe2179A9 that finally made it leave:

"Go away! Go away! *I hate you*!"

HfX7qe2179A9 was hated; there was no chance of ever connecting with the boy, no chance it would ever be one with the only creature for whom it had ever cared.

And now it was broken, missing an appendage.

As it turned away from the boy and left him sobbing on the floor, the remains of its arm melted down into a grey goo that ate away at the carpet and released a foul-smelling smoke. The decaying flesh had all but disintegrated by the time HfX7qe2179A9 reached the street and activated its signal-beacon for the return to its orbital pod.

There were two layover-vehicles above the planet's surface, orbital transfer-stations counter-rotating past each other in their respective hemispheres; the Queen's Hive-ship was in safer territory, on the far side of Mars, where it could more easily distance itself from the human's scout-ships. HfX7qe2179A9 had been to the Hive-ship only three times in its entire existence, and one of those had been its hatching. The other two were for rebuilding and repairing, patching the drone back together when its damages had been too extensive for the primitive restoration-facilities on the pods. The pods were hardly anything more than a place for the mobile units to park while they patched up minor leaks and uploaded their memory-banks to the Queen.

The wash. If it took refuge in the pod and didn't offer itself to the wash, the overseers would surely come for it. The overseers were mighty, warrior-caste, and nothing would save it if one of them were assigned to its destruction.

And there was another problem. The tissue-weavers aboard the pod had successfully stanched the loss of internal fluids but were entirely inadequate to reconstruct the lost arm. Its balance was barely affected, the arm had broken off just below the elbow so there was still plenty there to compensate for Earth-gravity, but...

The aesthetics were off. It didn't like the way it looked; it felt freakish, maladjusted.

The only realistic option was for HfX7qe2179A9 to risk effecting restorations aboard the Hive-ship; there was no other way, without attracting attention. Once there, it could potentially access the medi-bays and make repairs to itself, or even clone an entirely new mobile to indwell.

It would be aboard the same vessel as the Queen.

She was a being of extreme power, knowing intimately the thoughts of the entire Hive, even over vast distances. It wasn't sure it could maintain the shield of invisibility it had constructed in the hole between its thoughts; it wasn't sure of anything but its desire to stay alive. It had no other choice than to leave its fate up to chance.

There, between the nutrient-dispenser and the tissue-weaver, the flat panel with the grasping hooks that sucked its memories away, the rear occipital probes. It would have to briefly risk discovery in order to get transfer to the Hive-ship; it had to risk a little danger, in order to throw itself into the greatest danger of all. HfX7qe2179A9 backed up to the panel, allowing the synth-metal lancets to pierce into its skull and interface with its neural-net; the beacon was triggered, and it dissolved into a stream of dirty-light particles that whizzed off toward deep space, and the lurking Queen-Mother.

This was the first time HfX7qe2179A9 had been fully cognizant for its visit to the mother-ship; the shock of reintegration upon first arrival stayed with it long after its atoms had rearranged themselves on the receiver-pad. Where the pods had been largely bleak synth-metal, all grey paneling and ductwork, the Hive-ship appeared to be at least half-organic in origin, a living culture-vat stocked with a baffling array of fungi. In the receiving bay, HfX7qe2179A9 gathered itself and moved quickly away from the tele-pods, wary lest any new arrivals betray its presence with a mental image to be picked up by Her. It moved sideways in the shadows along the long, ribbed hallways, stumping out the light-pods where it crossed them and avoiding the busy junctures where there would be more of its kind. All visitors knew instinctively where to go, guided in their paths by the Queen's mental directives; HfX7qe2179A9, devoid of this internal prompting, wandered aimlessly until it lucked out and found an injured group of drones being escorted off for salvage by an overseer too busy to notice it. HfX7qe2179A9 maintained its distance and followed as closely as was possible.

When the overseer had finished sorting through the damaged mobiles and setting those aside who were beyond reconstitution, it left the others to take care of themselves and went off following other directives. HfX7qe2179A9 crept along the outermost edge of the chamber, beyond the range of detection by the self-absorbed drones attaching themselves to the repair apparatus, singling out a loner furthest from the rest of the group. For the first time in its existence, it summoned a fury which terrified it to the core and enabled the destruction of its prey. A gargling scream issuing from its beaked mouth, HfX7qe2179A9 raised its remaining claw and struck, driving its victim face-first into the doctoring machine, and then struck again, and continued striking until its prey struggled no more. Once finished, it discarded the husk in the great central recycle-vat and attached the usurped repairer to itself.

Microscopic hypodermic vesicles crawled over its membrane, ejecting themselves into its body and reconstructing the damaged mobile. In just a short time, HfX7qe2179A9 was whole again.

There was a noise from nearby—another overseer come to attend the recent batch of injured. The mobiles who'd been salvageable were all in various stages of self-maintenance, and those who couldn't be fixed were being cloned and re-loaded. The hexagonal clusters of their womb-tanks cast a deceptively sleepy orange glow that bustled with the activity of the pupae inside.

It was a blissful state of homeostasis, a type of immortality, purchased at the cost of individuality; those Hivelings who, through the proof of their service, were deemed worthy of reincarnation would be allowed to return indefinitely, so long as they were still serviceable and loyal. Occasionally a drone would be lost or destroyed—these were deemed failures and their fate recounted to the rest of the Hive as a cautionary tale. To be a self-managing drone, able to serve the Hive and Queen in a truly effective manner, one needed a finely-tuned and painstakingly-fortified consciousness, capable of taking orders and then understanding and carrying them out, possessed of the ability to construct logical arguments and to successfully reason through the particulars of complicated tasks. To maintain obedience and the true Hive-mentality required a unique process which the Overminds had mechanized and programmed into each clone's brain-stamp. HfX7qe2179A9 observed the hatchling mobiles gestating in the womb-tanks; watched the petty, mindless grubs mewling in their organic way to maturity; the sobbing, flabby grey hulks splatting wetly on the scaled floor as the vats were tipped out and descanted; the piercing cables socketed into place and the lights of a mobile's eye-sockets dimming as the brain-stamp imprinted the old drone onto its new body. HfX7qe2179A9 suspected that something had been stolen, and vowed never to let itself go through the process again.

The overseer finished with its ministrations, tapped the data input module mounted in the side of the wall, and left them again. HfX7qe2179A9 stepped cautiously from the shadows, intent upon checking the records of the report left by the overseer who'd just left for any mention of its intrusion, but was halted by its unexpected return. The giant bulk of the overseer's thorny carapace loomed before it, its scores of prehensile mandibles snapping in HfX7qe2179A9's face, the two-pronged mantis-claws twitching eagerly and dripping with venom.

HfX7qe2179A9 prepared to die; it would give fight, for as long as it could, but its death here was inevitable.

Then the unbelievable occurred; just as the monster's claws descended to pull HfX7qe2179A9's head from its body, the overseer froze in mid-attack. HfX7qe2179A9 could see the murderous intent and confused rage on the beast's photo-receptors, could smell its bloodlust and see it quivering with the effort to carry out its execution, but it had locked up completely, unable to move in any way. HfX7qe2179A9 reached forward with its newly-constructed arm and pushed the creature over; it dropped with a clatter to the floor and lay still, while HfX7qe2179A9 fell upon it and released a million lifetimes of pent-up rage.

Afterwards, the overseer scattered across the floor in pieces, HfX7qe2179A9 noticed a bruising over its hands and arms where it had contacted its enemies. HfX7qe2179A9 hauled all the pieces but one of the brute across the chamber and stuffed them into the recycle-vat, apprehensious about its new wounds: they would show, if it were seen, and it wouldn't have access to the repair-apparatus until another mobile came in with whom it could trade places. What these wounds signified, however, was much worse. Having just been on the rejuvenators, it should have been nigh invulnerable to all but the most grievous of injuries. Simple contact with a hard surface should never have left a mark—even the bottoms of its feet were bruising, where it stood upon the floor.

Nothing in HfX7qe2179A9's experience had prepared it to deal with its deterioration; if the mobile was damaged, it had the mobile repaired. Repairs were supposed to take, should last, barring some unforeseen tragedy.

It was still almost entirely new to the world of personal experience, and already that world was to be taken away from it. Now that it was at last allowed to retain any kind of individuality and memory outside of operational instinct, it would lose the container that held those traits together. Before, it had only to periodically surrender everything to the assimilatory wash and all those complications would have been solved for it.

The wash....

If anywhere there existed an answer to the dilemma which it now faced, HfX7qe2179A9 would be able to find that answer in the wash. Billions of years of experience, the collected knowledge of the entire Hive and every world and every species it had ever encountered, were reposited with the wash.

The rank and file were not permitted access to the vast library that was the wash; a drone such as HfX7qe2179A9 wasn't hard-wired to survive touching the stream of infinite knowledge, and the data-taps back on the pod functioned in such a way that the flow of information was entirely one-directional. The higher-caste mobiles alone were equipped to submerge themselves in the wash and come back with anything of themselves left, and then only those mobiles were outfitted as had need-to-know for their current objective. Only the overseers, and the Queen herself, were permanently wired with the ability. HfX7qe2179A9 would need to get inside the head of an overseer.

It just happened to have saved one.

HfX7qe2179A9 had recycled the dismembered corpse of the overseer who'd threatened its discovery, liquefying and rendering down into their basic proteins all parts but one—the head it'd saved, for the possible uses it could serve. Now it was to prove its usefulness.

A drone couldn't pull information from the wash, but an overseer could, and an overseer could act as go-between for the drone and remotely access that information on its behalf, wirelessly effecting a transfer that wouldn't blow out the drone's memory-banks.

HfX7qe2179A9 extended its retractable thumb-claw and peeled the leathery skin back from the overseer's skull. The gold wires that permeated the creature's brain rode up at the base of the skull, where they interfaced with a small glowing chip of a heavy crystalline element condensed deep in the vacuum of space. All the wiring appeared to be intact and the glowing chip pulsed regularly, giving every indication of functionality. There was a separate cluster of the golden wires that connected directly to a gland in the overseer's forebrain; HfX7qe2179A9 carefully separated these wires from the rest and then severed them neatly. Now the creature would be unable to mentally contact the Queen.

HfX7qe2179A9 dragged the head across the floor of the chamber to where the rejuvenators were situated, carefully attaching one of the IV-sustainers to the overseer's protruding spinal-stump. The machine's questing nano-probes sucked greedily at the exposed nerves and melded with the discarded body-part, lending it artificial animation. The overseer's head winked into life and its eyes rolled crazily in its sockets as it fought to gain control over its situation. Powerless, it attempted to physically scream, but without lungs was breathless. At last convinced of its handicap, it turned its full attention on its captor. HfX7qe2179A9 felt the waves of the creature's indomitable will striking against its consciousness, attempting to wrest control of its mobile away from it, but resisted the command to succumb. The head tried strike after strike against it, but HfX7qe2179A9 refused each new assault more easily than it had the last, until the head had fully exhausted itself; then HfX7qe2179A9 reached out to it with its thumb-claw and popped one of the overseer's eyeballs. The head was now ready to take commands.

Chapter 5: ***Collateral Damages And Unacceptable Loss***

The Hive-queen was duly impressed with the manner in which the drone had taken control of its new situation; it was only recently that it had gained sentience, and already it had come home seeking Her knowledge. She was still, at this stage, allowing it to act freely, so that She could observe and study what it would do and how it would handle its new freedom; She'd even assisted it when Her overseer had threatened to bring the drone's antics to a halt.

And now it was using those remains to know Her mind.

The drone sought predictable information; it had apparently discovered its deteriorating state. Sooner or later, all those who'd gained sentience sought answers to why their mobiles fell apart; it was a question pursued in every civilization She'd encountered. None had answered it, yet. She let the drone peruse meaningless realms of gene-code data, endless spiels of nucleotide-tables, the ebb and flow of cellular cycles; none of it would prove meaningful. The mantids pored over the data ceaselessly, had done so for millennia, without any result of significance. Still, She allowed the little drone the opportunity to satisfy its budding curiosity and give up that pursuit of its own accord.

And then, once again, it went with predictable actions; this time it had chosen to peruse some of the Hive's more recent priorities, probably looking for itself, to see whether it had been discovered. She took a few directives away, moving them to priority-trees beyond its access, preventing the drone from sharing that particular information, and then returned to observing its actions in the data-wash.

Now it was doing something interesting.

It had discovered a minor directive, pertaining to a human who'd slipped the net. Such event, while not a common occurrence, merited only a low-priority status; this human was strictly non-element, having only a simple memory-lock and psi-dampening in place. It hardly registered, in terms of human affairs, and yet the drone was offering it aid, had loosened the memory-lock and initiated a positive psi-current, one that would have the effect of increasing the human's willpower-returns and counteracting an interference-trend thrown upon it by other humans, at Her order.

The drone was issuing its own orders, directly countering Her own!

The moment passed, and She allowed the creature to continue what it was doing. Perhaps something interesting would come of it.

Jeremy recovered; the past day and a half had been the leaky, furious hell of recurrent influenza, a punitive slap through the head with an acid-filled dirty sock. He'd lain in bed the entire time, soaking the sheets with his misery, which was only broken by Maria's periodic visits, when she came to check up on him and offer medicinal teas. He refused to drink any of them.

"How can I help you if you won't let me? There's only so much I can really do to help you. Let me do what I can for you. You know, it won't hurt you to drink the tea." Maria was growing short with him.

"It's not tea I need. I just need to get whatever this is out of my body and I'll be fine again."

"That's what I'm talking about. This will help."

"Look, I..... I'm fine. I'm feeling better already."

"Jeremy, it's all you. Whatever you want." She turned away.

"Go on, just leave it on the coffeetable. I'll be fine, really."

Maria sat quietly for a breath, nodded, "You're pretty sick. I saw some cold-pills in your medicine cabinet earlier, would you like some?"

"Aggh, yes I would. Thank you."

She left his side and went to the bathroom, returning a minute later with a pill-bottle.

"Damn, this child-proof cap is a real beast!"

She fumbles the bottle and it rolls under the bed, coming to rest against an old shoe-box.

"Oh, shoot. I've dropped it."

She goes down on one knee and peers beneath the futon, sighting the dropped bottle.

"Hey, what's in the box?"

She smiles playfully at him while reaching under the bed and pulling out the items: a rolled-up poster in a cardboard tube, half a bottle of soda pop, the shoe-box, two mismatched dirty socks, a videogame-controller...

"Hey, there's something else under here...."

Her hand closes around the block of urgomite and brings it out into the light.

"What is that?" he asks, rubbing at his eyes.

"It's that stuff your teacher-friend gave you."

"Stuff, what stuff?"

"That—that burgermite, or whatever he called it. Here, take it."

"What do you want me to do with it?"

"Just take it. Keep it with you."

"Why?"

"I've got a good feeling about this. Humor me, okay? Just hang on to it for a couple days at least. Maybe it'll help; at the worst, it couldn't do any harm. Go on, you know you wanna take it."

"Put it in my coat pocket. I take that with me pretty much any time I go out anywhere. It'll always be close by if you stick it in one of my pockets. I've got a lot of junk in there."

Jeremy's pockets are loaded with change, gum-packets, toothpicks, dice, marbles, superballs, matchbooks, spools of thread, pencil-stubs, nail-clippers, paper-clips, rubber bathtub-stopper, flashlight, walkman radio, bus-schedule, bible tracts, pocket-knife, postcards, business-cards, stamps, safety-pins, bottle-opener, a yellow rubber duckie. "Ah, God, how do you deal with your stuff, if you got all this junk in the way? Seriously, it's like the Salvation Army in here."

The block of urgomite touches the other objects in the pocket, infusing them with an acceleration of the atomic spin; the effect is subtle, where once they clattered together, they now tinkle.

"Yeah, just leave it in there, and don't mess with any of my things. I use that stuff."

"Yeah, you don't worry about that. There you go."

"What are you doing messing around in my pockets, anyway? There's nothing in there for you."

The charged particles of the urgomite emanate a field of resonant disorganization, condensating and collapsing the darker, slower energy-bands and precipitating them out of the environment: as the wave of pulsation expands outward from the block, all the dust drops out of the air at once with a hint of ozone wafting on the breeze.

"Don't I know it. You can keep your pocket-junk."

They go on in the same way, not really saying much to each other, for a further ten minutes until Maria comes to her senses and leaves.

Jeremy sits up in his bed, puts his coat on over his pajamas, and shivers.

The block settles in amongst his junk and miscellanea, and continues to work its magic.

Jeremy breathed in the radiations and began his metamorphosis.

An entire day passed without Jeremy seeing Maria again, then two, and still he didn't try to call her. Instead, he sat contented with his misery and abandonment by himself, writhing with the cold, stinging burn of her absence but refusing to give in, a stoic; he would not fall prey to the same fever of his last episode just for the attention, not this time. Let her wait it out.

He went to work, skipped his classes, and sat up late at nights with his hands full of muddy clay, forming in his mind shapes that differed from the shapes the clay took, ugly misrepresentations of his desire. Art, once again, was not to be his refuge.

And then the phone rang; it was *her*. The other one.

It was Laylah.

She was quick on the telephone, near-breathless: "Jeremy, I have to see you. Something's happened. I need to see you right away."

He allowed her back to his apartment and listened to her tale of woe while she shifted about in her seat. Her sister had appeared suddenly on the scene out of nowhere and stolen her husband away from her, taking the car, house and money and everything else, leaving her on her own to fend for herself. For the first time in fourteen years, she was frightfully alone and utterly without any support network. She'd come to realize in the time she'd been away that Jeremy was the most important person in her life and that she'd been terribly unkind to him by not returning to him right away and staying by his side as she should have. Jeremy told her that he'd been seeing another girl, that he thought he really liked her and wanted to be with her, and she relented, easing away from him and cooing greasily, "Ohh, I understand. She's a very lucky girl, a very lucky girl, indeed." She twirled her finger in Jeremy's hair, above his ear.

"Where is this girl now?" She asked.

"I don't know. I haven't talked to her in a few days, since I was sick."

"Aww, she disappeared when you were sick? That's terrible. I'd never do that to you. Let's go outside. I want to look at the stars."

She took his hand and led him to the door; he stopped,

pulling against her and turning away. She did not let him go.

"I just need my coat..."

"Leave it. We'll only be out here for a short while."

He went outside with her, to the porch, and looked up at the night sky. There was a single light, brighter than the others, tracking slowly against the speckled firmament and winking at him with evil intent. She continued past him.

"Come on, let's get in my car. There's a heater in it, we don't have to be cold."

"Ehh, I'm not sure..."

"Come on, I'm not parked very far away. I'm just down on the street here. We can turn on the heater, it'll be fun. Come on."

She pulled him into her car; he let her.

Of course, she fired the engine and started driving away.

"Where are we going?"

"I don't know, I just wanted to get out of that stuffy room. That playdough or whatever it was you were goofing around with stank. I needed the fresh air."

"But where are we driving to, is what I was asking."

"I don't know. I have a sub-let apartment I'm staying in now. It's nothing permanent, it's just until I get back on my feet. You want to see my new apartment? Sure, let's go there!"

Jeremy didn't say much on the freeway, against the blinking lights of passing semis and the flickering in the dashboard from a shorting bulb; he counted the passage of time and distance from his apartment, the telephone, the chance that Maria might be calling. He was pretty sure he was cheating on her, or close enough to it. Being in Laylah's presence felt obscene to him.

She took him to her apartment, showed him a comfortable couch, and gave him alcohol. She did not allow him to see the powder she mixed into his cup; she pushed him to drink more and kept them coming. A fog began eating his surroundings and her manner changed, becoming more pitched, angled at him, a spider preparing to cocoon.

Jeremy finds himself suddenly short of breath; dizzy lights spin before his eyes and the walls won't stay still, threatening to push his stomach up through his throat. He closes his eyes and grips the sides of the couch, daring the world to stop its convulsions long enough for him to step off; the strobing patterns he sees behind his eyelids swim vertiginously, engulfing him with their agonizing brightness.

He thinks of Maria again, of what he's endangering by being here with Laylah, and something in his chest begins to burn in time to the singing lights. There is, he sees, no other way to get past the swirling oblivion swimming up to meet him than to embrace it, let it be heard, and allow its message to deliver him to the other side. A stream of fleeting images passes before him: Maria in the ice-cream parlor, laughing as she touches his hand; Maria and Mister Peabody smiling at him as they invite him to join their conversation; Maria lying beneath him on his bed calling his name in ecstasy. The feelings of warmth he has for her are the only thing keeping him tethered to the ground, all that stays the fire in his chest from consuming him. That heat, coalescing on the lines attaching his heart to his head, condenses into a single cord of flame burning him away utterly and leaving all impurities behind. When he hears the ringing bells, a pealing of the angelic chorale, an easiness falls upon him and he relaxes back into his couch, Laylah going to him to express her concern.

Now she puts her hand upon his chest: was he alright?

Jeremy takes her hand in his own and says, "I think so. For a moment I thought I was going to pass out. I'm okay now."

Then she asks him: "How would you like to get into bed? Do you need to lie down? How about I get you in bed?"

The pulsing purple-yellow darkness comes again, encroaching on his vision and taking the sharp details out of objects; Jeremy grips the side of the couch: "No, I'm fine right here."

She gets close to him: "Are you sure? How about I at least take off your shoes..."

She sits down on the ground in front of him, putting her

hand on his knee, and tugs a shoelace. Her face is masklike with practiced seduction: the coy feigning of surprise and pleasure, the playful wink as she removes his shoe, the batting eyelashes as she takes the other shoe off. Something in her smouldering look of promise hooks Jeremy and he feels an answering warmth in his loins, his recently-acquired power rushing away to his lap. He tries to sit up:

"Where are you going? Sit back down, until you tell me where you're going."

"I need some water."

"Hold on, I'll get you some water. Stay right there."

She leaves, comes back with a glass of water and he's still there, sitting where she left him.

"I couldn't get to my shoes. I don't feel right. Can I lay down someplace?"

"Of course you can."

She brushes up against him, putting her arm on his chest: "I've got everything you'll need."

"Can you close the curtains? That flashing light is bothering me." He waves his arm at the window, in the direction of the newly-erected radio-tower.

She leaves him wincing on the couch and covering his eyes to go shut the curtain: "The cable company just put in the new transmitter. They said we'd get better reception but my cel-phone doesn't work for shit... My internet's terrible out here, too. I only use it when I go into town."

She wrestles with the tangled cords of the venetian blinds, tugging the beige plastic slats down to block the sight of the flashing red eye atop the repeater-tower. "There you go. Are you sure I can't get you something to drink, maybe something else, with a little bit of kick? I've got some pills—"

But the words are lost in the roar of a passing semi; the shelves shake, dishes clatter in the cupboards, picture-frames rattle on the wall. Her voice is drowned out and from a black box on her tiny desk blares forth an electronic trumpet, "Five-seven *run* niner."

"What the hell?"

"It's just my answering machine. It acts up sometimes when someone's using a CB-radio outside. You should hear it squall when the police are around. I don't know why it does that."

"I don't....feel well. I'm just going to close my eyes for a little bit..."

Laylah leans in reaching, a half-step taken towards him in the space of a single breath, her tongue darting over her lips: "Are you sure I can't give you a little something? Don't you want to stay up and party with me? Come on, let's party!"

She leans over him to tease his hair, brushes his shoulder with her breast, but his eyes are closed and he's asleep before his head hits the armrest.

There are people with him at the fire-pit on top of the wooded hill. They had come through the ritual of the blood and were ready to disband and follow other pursuits. His family and two others were going down to the farmhouse at the bottom of the hill; they were going to the giant double-smelters, where the body would be burnt.

A loud voice yelled "Forget!"

Jeremy looked back to the farmhouse. Its ancient wooden slats and iron horseshoes nailed to the wall proclaimed it to be a family homestead, a generational land-inheritance kept in working repair, if not actively used for subsistence-living. The double-smelters were the most modern equipment in the building, a pair of pre-world war one behemoths used in the early steel-mills, out-of-place artifacts stored in the outbuilding and only used in the most terrible of circumstances.

They were smouldering now, belching out gouts of black smoke into the dusking sky, a low-hanging haze that choked with mildewing timber and a caustic sulphur-based stink that irritated the eyes.

They'd brought the dead girl's body down from the top of the hill. She'd been hacked into pieces, mutilated savagely. They'd dropped her remains in front of the smelters, and then a man lit the antique tanks and stuffed her inside. The burning took a long time and smelled awful; when everything had been reduced to ash, the oldest man pressed his finger into the white powder and ran it down Jeremy's forehead.

The ringing telephone woke him to the darkness of the unlit room. It seemed like the awful racket had been going on forever, dragging him out of the horrible dream and pummeling him into an upright position. No one came to answer it and so he waited it out for twelve, fifteen rings, with his head pounding and the taste of sick in his mouth. On the twentieth he forced himself to his feet, with a muttering of 'Why doesn't the damn answering machine pick up?' He took the phone off its cradle and put it to his ear.

There was an electric screech, followed by a hiss, and then a voice said, clearly, "You need to get home, Mister Proctor," before the line went dead.

"Hello? Hello?" Jeremy was dumbfounded.

Laylah came into the room, wearing only a long button-down shirt. "I heard a noise. What are you doing up? Are you feeling any better?"

"Why doesn't anyone answer the phone here?"

"Forget about that now. Why don't you come to bed? Just forget about that and come to bed."

"I don't feel very good." His headache was pounding in time to the red lights blinking around the slates of the venetian shades.

"Honestly, Jeremy, I don't know what's wrong with you. Why don't you go to bed with me? Am I disgusting?"

"How did the people on the phone know I was here? How did they know my name?"

"Forget about all that. Come to bed with me, now."

"I have a headache. I want to go home now."

"Uggh. I'll take you in the morning. Last chance to change your mind."

"Fine, I'll sleep on the couch. I don't think I should be here."

"Suit yourself. If you change your mind, you can still come in if you want."

Jeremy slept the rest of the night on the couch, alone.

He rose early and pulled the shades open to catch the rising sun, and the penetrating lights of the large framework tower across the lot from him stabbed through the slats. There were birds squawking somewhere, but none of them were to be found nesting in its iron perches. Jeremy watched the sun rise with his hand to his temple. *All night long* he could feel the tattooing of the winking light on the backs of his eyelids, felt his body jumping in time to its music, made up songs that fit the rhythm of the pounding microwave-surf:

"*When* the *lamp* of *night* goes *out*,

"*There's* no *need* to *fret* a-*bout*!"

The idiot phrase ran circles in his head endlessly, driving the passage of time to hyper-crawl, the song locked into his mind irrevocably. Minutes burned with the slow heat of aeons, the mantra droning in precision verse, metronomic and omnipresent. He'd woken with it still stuck in his head, as if it weren't bad enough to have fallen asleep to it. He'd even come up with a second verse:

"*All* the *world* is *in* your *head*,

"And *eve*-ry-*bo*-dy *wants* you *dead*."

He wasn't sure where the words were coming from—it wasn't a very nice or comforting sentiment to have running circles in one's mind, even if it was kinda familiar. He was hearing voices in his head, snatches of foreign languages he didn't understand, strings of numbers...

The raging fires of the smelters burned in his nostrils; the stench of the dead covered *everything*...

His world was shaking up.

Laylah came back into the room, her hair disheveled and her makeup smearing down her face.

"You didn't come. What time is it? What are you doing here still?"

Jeremy didn't have an immediate answer for her. "I fell asleep on your couch. I don't know what time it is. Early morning. That thing over there kept me up all night."

As he pointed at the tower, glowing in the dawn, the first

direct sunlight fell on the lamp's sensors, and the red lantern blinked off for the last time.

"I don't see why it should bother you. It's just a little blinking light."

"Can't you feel it in your head? Uggh, I have a terrible headache."

"Maybe you should take a couple of pills and go. I need to get ready for work."

"I don't need any pills. I'll go now."

He crossed the room uncomfortably, shouldered past her and to the door, pulling his collar up as he pulled on the handle.

"I'll come by your place tonight. There's still something I need to talk to you about, something important."

"Uhh, okay." He didn't know what else to say; Jeremy wasn't thinking clearly, but there was something yet about the idea that set off warning bells.

Without further reply, he went outside and shut the door on her, closing off Laylah and that aspect of his life. He walked away from her at a pace just shy of a run, seeking the street and the sanctuary of movement. He was guilty deep-down, he knew it, of infidelity to Maria; he'd spent the night at another woman's house, an ex-girlfriend. It couldn't be acceptable.

And she hadn't even offered him a ride home in the morning.

Dawn was crisp and he walked quickly, squinting into the morning light; the streets ahead were choked with traffic, people going places in a hurry, impatient and surly. There was a long line of cars behind a semi-truck at a stoplight, and none of the drivers seemed to be particularly pleased about it. The light turned in his favor to cross the street and he jogged across the intersection, nodding at the driver of the big truck as he passed under the grille. The driver didn't give any acknowledgment.

Someone rolled down their car-window; there was a stereo playing inside, at full volume, a gangster's wheels with a pimped-out stereo. They were listening to rap, the DJ a male voice with a gravelly snarl, deep-throated and lewd:

"...and when I'm done you know I'm gonna *get the fuck out of there!*"

The beat was still bumping at its established dull roar, but the last words were uncommonly accented, a pitch lower and higher simultaneously, and twice as loud as any other noise on the street.

Jeremy picked up his pace and hustled down the sidewalk, the hairs on the back of his neck standing on end.

The light changed, and the semi started a wide turn to follow down the street behind him. It was slow going through the clustered traffic and the cars behind it started honking their horns.

The street unrolled before him like a long ribbon, stretching off to the far distance of the horizon, its end lost in the brownish haze of smog. A car peeled out with a screech of rubber from around a corner and bore down upon him. Jeremy picked up his pace again, eyes darting up and down the street for a bus to catch or maybe even an open doorway...

The driver of the car barely missed him and careened into the truck; the crunch of metal was like a bowl of solid sound collapsing around his head, near deafening and ringing with destruction and mayhem.

There was the distinct cough of a CB-radio, and a monotone voice interrupted: "Copy. Subject evaded."

Then the envelope of sound disengaged and the rest of the world came crashing in; the honking horns, the shouting and the yelling, the approach of distant sirens, the city in outrage. Jeremy skipped along the sidewalk, not wanting to be involved in any kind of accident-reportage.

Jeremy started to run.

He first noticed that his headache had gone when he'd gotten to within a few blocks of his home. There was marked improvement upon sighting his front door, and by the time he was inside, he felt practically normal again. Jeremy decided that he wouldn't tell Maria about the night before—but he wasn't willing to go so far as to tell her an outright lie, if she did ask. There wasn't anything to tell, really. Not when you looked at it right.

He'd spent the night on a friend's couch; he was far from home and too sick to move, so it wasn't anyone's fault. And he kept himself to himself; he hadn't messed around or cheated on her, or anything. He'd been good; in fact, you could have said that he was there in the first place doing his friend a favor, so that made him look even better.

But he'd keep that point to himself; it wasn't a boast he'd throw out there, unless it had to come up.

He went to work; he went to class. It was pretty much the same as any other day, apart from the heart-breaking, languishing agony of guilt and the dread, knowing that this would surely drive the final nail in the coffin awaiting the death of his relationship with Maria. She hadn't talked to him for a week now, maybe longer. He didn't care—that was what he kept telling himself.

That night, as she'd said, Laylah called him.

The ringing telephone surprised him; he wasn't used to getting many calls, almost none of them good, and he'd hoped fretfully that it was Maria.

Laylah's voice licked against his ear, enunciating like a squirtgun. "I'm coming over. There's something I need to tell you."

Jeremy was quick, bound not to let her hang up without first relinquishing something. "What do you need to tell me that you can't do over the phone?"

"I'll tell you when I get there. See you in fifteen."

She hung up; there was a crackle of static in the earpiece, and Jeremy put the phone back on its base.

She arrived exactly twenty-four minutes later, looking uncomfortable and out of breath.

"What's going on here? What do you have to tell me?"

"Just come outside with me. It's stuffy in here."

"No, I fell for that before. What do you want? What do you have to say that's so 'important'?"

She hesitated; then, "I... can't say. Come away with me Jeremy, it'll be like we always wanted it to be... Just come *outside with me.*"

Their wills locked, tousled; Jeremy held his own. "Nah, I think I better not."

"Fine. I'll go then." She stood in the open doorway, statuesque and waiting. Jeremy took hold of the door, ready to pass the bolt after her.

She grabbed his arm and pulled him into her; she made herself soft for him, wrapping him in her scent. He stiffened against her, but her mouth had already sought his and her tongue pressed sweet fluids against his teeth. Jeremy noticed a change in the background hiss and saw Maria coming up the street to his door and, oh yes, she'd seen them. It was over quicker than he'd known.

Laylah passed by Maria with a raised eyebrow, and that was probably the moment that decided the rest of their short future together. Maria didn't look happy. Laylah had done her job.

"Who was that?" Jeremy gave her the name. "She's the woman in all those paintings you showed me, isn't she?"

"I can't compete with *that*!"

Maria was out of his life that fast.

She'd said other things, too, with less gravity and more platitudes, telling him she thought they'd be better as friends; then her words took on a more critical edge. She told him he was carrying too much baggage around to be a good choice for her boyfriend, and that she needed a certain kind of person to be with.

And like that, Jeremy was alone again.

Chapter 6: ***Holding Hands With Death***

The back of his neck was sore. There was a pinprick, then blackness.

Tom woke up periodically throughout his experience, brief flashing incoherent visions that didn't string together. At one point, he was sure he was in a hospital surrounded by doctors in white smocks and military men in dark suits. They were feeding him a mash that tasted like bananas, telling him to eat it for his country. He was sure the mash would kill him, that it was poison, but he ate it anyway. He didn't know what else to do.

At another point, he seemed to be in some kind of pool or giant fishtank; there were several other people in scuba-gear in the tank with him, and a dolphin. Bundles of cabling dragged through the waters like seaweed; they connected him somehow to the dolphin, and the scuba-men were removing them from the tank. The dolphin looked deep into his eyes and uttered a piercing trill that shook him from inside. He fought against the wires attached to his head, and the scuba-men turned their attention on him.

The next thing he remembered, Tom woke up on the left side of his double king-sized bed; his girlfriend had woken before him. He could smell the coffee brewing.

This was the life: an early breakfast with... What was her name? Linda? Carol? It was right on the tip of his tongue, funny he shouldn't remember it... Then off to work, doing... What did he do?

Something was wrong here. There seemed to be too many holes in his memory...

He woke up alone in his double king-sized bed; he could already smell the coffee brewing.

It was one of those 'smart' models, with a built-in clock-timer. He'd set it the night before. He'd had an appointment early in the morning and wouldn't have had time to mess around with it. If he didn't hurry, he'd be late.

He got his car out of the garage, kissed his wife through the window, and pulled out of the driveway; his wife was a picture of the American Ideal in his rearview-mirror, with her apron around her waist and her hair put up in a bun, come out to the street with him to see him off and awaiting his return. He saluted her reflection, straightened his tie, and drove to the office.

It was another day of paperwork.

Spreadsheets, bar-graphs, statistical analyses—it was easier if you didn't consciously think about it, if you just let your mind drift while your eyes picked out the answers and your hand recorded them. It was actually better *not* to think about the process, but rather to stand aside and let it happen.

He watched himself fill reams of paper with meaningless numbers, his fingers flying over the keypad, building a pattern he dared not observe. After a while, he checked the clock—eight hours had passed. It must be time to go home. He shut down the computer, collected the pile of paper from the printer, turned off the lights, and left the office.

As he approached the large bay windows in the main lobby, a bird flew into the glass and stuck there, flapping its wings in a mad attempt to enter the foyer. Tom watched it curiously as he left the building, then promptly forgot about it as he crossed the parking lot. The inside of his car smelled like fish.

"What's going on here?" he asked no one in particular.

His car wouldn't start; the engine turned over but the ignition didn't want to catch. He smacked the steering wheel and cursed, then tried keying it again.

This time the car sprang into life.

He drove home—traffic was thin and agreeable. He made it back in excellent time. Things were looking a little better already.

His boyfriend was waiting for him at the door. Alex's hair was wet—he must have just gotten out of the shower. He looked angry and impatient. Maybe things weren't as peachy as he'd thought they were. The office, for all its endless hours of sterile repetition, was looking nostalgic by comparison.

He got out of his car slowly, laboriously. He caught himself dragging his heels and wondered if his and Alex's relationship wasn't running itself out to an end. Alex looked like he was getting ready to start yelling at him again for something. The door was a million miles away and advancing with the lethal inevitability of a glacier. Alex was getting ready to yell at him.

"For a given set of vectors x, y, z and q, what is the conjugal phase-space of coordina—" Alex choked off.

Tom sat on the couch.

His name was Tom.

Something was wrong, very wrong.

His world was ending, again.

No more Maria, and he'd just turned Laylah away.

He'd screwed everything up *again*. He punched the air.

Jeremy paced his apartment, livingroom to bedside to kitchen to livingroom to bedside and on and on and on. The wind howled outside, indicative of his mood. He'd blown it.

He could kick high, with force, a perfect extension of his anger. He chopped invisible opponents, punched them in their vital spots. There were so many times he'd screwed things up, so many failures in his past he'd been unable to keep count. For a time, life had handed him opportunity after golden opportunity, and he'd botched them all, one after the other. He had no power to make his dreams real. It hurt, thinking about all the time he'd spent not living up to his expectations of himself. Not to mention the expectations of others. He couldn't do *anything* right. Life was his enemy. The last slash of his invisible sword was aimed at his own heart. Something in his pocket hummed neutrally, and Jeremy's racing mind quieted to a dull roar.

Finally, he worked himself down enough to take off his jacket. He was at home; he could at least try to get comfortable. He changed his mind; he needed it, the security that vigilance brought. It wasn't time to relax just yet. Something unnameable impelled him from within.

The apartment was feeling too small; what he needed was a walk, to clear his head. It was windy, but the cool air riffing past and through him brought the clarity of mind he needed. The evening was still warm, enough so that he knew if he walked at any kind of pace, he'd soon be too hot. He probably wouldn't need any of his stuff, either; he didn't really care so much about it anymore. What good was stuff, if there was no one worthwhile to share it with? In the end he decided to take it with him. You never knew.

The world was a treacherous place; it required 'special dispensations' to deal with it.

If that meant you had to hustle a little bit here while you shuffled a little bit there, if someone got hurt or was left behind so that you could get ahead, it meant in the long run you'd be alright. The important thing was the bigger picture, and the things you had to do were just the things you had to do.

"The things you had to do were just thing things you had to do..." It made a recurrent song in his head, looping over and over in time to the crosswalk-lights, blinking the tempo; tick, tick, tick.

A tic; another voice in his head drew to the fore wanting him to get up and get mad. There was so much to get angry about, so *much*...

Mongoose checked the controls; the rad-table for the last sequence he'd run was starting to show some results. At last, something was beginning to take hold. Too bad he wasn't supposed to be pursuing it any more.

The kid had let himself be compromised, had given him an opening by consorting with the RomInt, and now he had a niggling edge that could be tweaked with the proper persuasion. If he didn't let the kid slip him this time, he might be able to redeem himself in the eyes of his superiors. Assuming they didn't court-martial him.

But the kid...

The kid vexed him, and he could always claim he was just following orders, just following orders. They probably wouldn't double-check the time-tables, and even if they did it would only show him as being someone who followed through. He'd been told to eliminate the subject, and he had.

Let the kid's folly drag him to hell; the kid's loss was his gain.

Somewhere behind him a streetlamp fizzled and popped out loudly, shrouding his building in shadow. Jeremy barely noticed; he had other concerns.

He couldn't keep his legs moving fast enough to keep pace with his racing thoughts. If he couldn't focus on them, it was because they came at such a rate that they slid into one another and lost their individuality, like the single cells of a film-strip becoming a moving picture. His thoughts were fluid, roiling magma that caught everything on fire, igniting a world with the rage of a dark god. If before he'd failed, he'd come back again, fighting with the violence of angels; his whirlwind took out all before it in a storm of retribution.

His whole life he'd been other peoples' doormat. This was about to change. Something was goading him; he felt euphoric, giddy on revenge and dark armors, the newfound heartlessness of the assassin. This was *life*; this was *power*.

This was a thing he had to do. He needed to start living his life the way he needed to live it, and he had to take care of what was important to *him*. He needed to take care of *himself* for a change.

He was restless; he needed something to *do*.

There was a bookstore nearby; it was the closest landmark for several blocks, and only a short walk away from his home. He liked it for that reason. If he didn't meet up with someone who'd screwed him over in the past, then at least he could try to find something interesting to read. If he *did* find someone who needed a piece of his mind, however, then they were sure to get it.

And then a strange thing happened:

For just a second, he was looking out a different set of eyeballs; from his new vantage-point, he was looking down at a freshly-shaved pair of female legs, examining the sheen of drying lotion and thinking about how to snag a certain man. Everything about this woman felt of Laylah, smelled of Laylah, resounded with her touch, and when she looked up at herself in the bathroom mirror a second later, just before breaking contact, Jeremy looked into her familiar features and saw himself gazing back from the reflections of her pupils.

Just as quickly as it had come, the vision was gone. Jeremy wondered if he were going crazy, and then immediately dismissed the episode and forgot it had ever happened, stepping off the curb to cross the street and enter the store.

He didn't see anyone he recognized there, and the books were a disappointing selection of used paperbacks on black magick.

He picked one up at random, a black paperback volume with red lettering.

Magick with a 'k'. Pretentious crap.

He flipped through the pages; it was all a bunch of 'please gimme', if you really thought about it. Stupid stuff. Just for laughs, he thought he'd try reading out loud some of the gibberish. Would other people hear him? Did he care?

Funnily enough, the syllables rolled naturally off his tongue, a stranger's voice in his larynx mouthing foreign words in an archaic and forgotten dialect. There was a tickle in his throat, and a definite sensation that his head was splitting in two, or that his eyes were looking in opposing directions. A streamer of something plasmic rose from Jeremy's head and shoulders and split itself, pulling the world in different directions.

The wind outside raised to a tempestuous howl.

Jeremy cleared his throat; a bolt of lightning lit the sky; he continued to read the words out. It was all a joke, right? He didn't care if other people thought he was being stupid, it didn't matter.

There was a warmth against his hip; he continued reading the barbarous incantation, oblivious to the wind now penetrating the bookstore with a faint reek of sulphur. Thunder cracked, and the warmth at his hip started to become unbearable, shaking loose the book's grasp on him. The two other customers in the store with him fled.

"Hey buddy, you're scaring off business! Give me that!"

Jeremy let the man take the book from his unresisting hands. The heat in his pocket eased off, letting him concentrate on a complete return to his senses.

"Now get out of here! And don't ever come back!" The store-manager was severely displeased. Jeremy left the bookshop in a daze, stepping over spilled textbooks on his way out. It was one more to add to a string of losses.

He stumbled out onto the road; how was he going to get home? Where the hell *was* home anyway?

A man bumped into him, going into the bookstore, a man all in black with the suit and the mirror-shades and the derby. It was just enough to unnerve him, this image of the archetypal G-man, but he barely said a word and didn't look back. Jeremy had the feeling he'd run under a giant, sweeping eye and been somehow missed.

Something was trying to get his attention; something was amiss with his trip to the bookstore. The heat.

He patted himself down about the hips, taking into account the feel of his inner workings, and found a lump in his jacket pocket.

It was the block of urgomite, the one *she'd* asked him to hold—his last and only true love.

The walk home from the bookstore from which he'd just been barred had shown him that; Laylah was meaningless to him, was probably only hanging around him because things weren't working out with her husband again. She didn't have any *real* interest in Jeremy and probably never had. It was another wound. Burning waves of shame engulfed him and he wanted to strike out at something, anything; he almost hurled the little block of metal and plastic away from him, but thought better of it at the last moment and put it back in his pocket. If nothing else, it would serve as a reminder to him, to watch out for vicious women.

He'd never understood his initial interest in Laylah; it had gone quickly to obsession, overly preoccupying his conscious thoughts so that he found himself imagining her all day and all night. Something about her seemed intensely familiar; he'd even brought it up to her, once, but neither of them had any idea of where they could possibly have met up before. He was just as strange to her as she was to him, but for Jeremy the question ran deeper, taking over his mind and driving him with the need to place her in his past.

He found his way home, and collapsed down into the warm comforting depths of his couch—the remote was just up on the coffee-table, within arm's reach... It wouldn't be 'doing' anything, but it might help to take his mind off his problems, if only for a bit.

He turned the TV on.

There were riots in the capitol city, and Springfield, and Dayton. The state of Pennsylvania was aflame, and Belize had been flattened in an earthquake. The damage was total.

He changed the channel, quickly; more news about the riots—it seemed like everybody was focused on the unrest. It gave him a headache.

The warmth against the side of his legs brought him to attention. There was a tickling, not altogether unpleasant, that drew him out of his fugue-state.

He reached into his pocket; it was coming from the urgomite.

As he held the block of plastic and metal in his hand and gazed into its depths, he caught a split-second glimpse of a hazy, whitish cloud exploding from the block in a donut-shape, and then it was gone. He couldn't even be sure if he'd actually seen it.

And then, just as suddenly, he became aware of a clattering, ratcheting screech that had been coming from the walls and ceiling of his apartment; he'd only just noticed it, but it felt to him like the noise had been going on forever.

When he listened closely, it seemed to be the most concentrated in the furthest corner by his balcony, so he stepped outside to look for possible sources of the noise and immediately caught sight of the tower on the hillside, the blinking red lights keeping time with the racket in his head. Damn, the things were *everywhere*!

He held the shiny block, clamped his fingers around it and closed his eyes with concentration; a wave of electricity cascaded from his spine, down his arm and into the urgomite, and the noise subsided. It was a triumph of will. It might have been purely a subjective experience, but he couldn't deny the reality of what had happened to him. *Something* in him was changing; he was beginning to see behind the curtain.

The call came through to Agent MON2985's chip, the cranial-link reserved for high-command or emergency-broadcasts; there was a breach-signal recorded at a bookstore, a Sigma-spectral event, and he was required to respond immediately. This was definitely becoming a habit with him, this sudden changing of plans. Some part of him ached to be allowed to grouch about it, but he pushed the irritability aside. It was his job; it was his duty to his country.

Still, it would be nice if someone could make up their fucking minds. Which head of the hydra was giving the fucking orders *now*?

The bookstore was in a shambles, etherically-speaking. The constructs that made up its topography were faded and even torn in places; the kid had done a real number on the joint. In this ultraviolet spectrum, what should have looked like any other low-rent retail outlet appeared at broken angles, decayed, torn asunder and crawling with chitinous insects. The breach was severe; if not corrected soon, the entire premises would rapidly degrade into an abandoned zone, a cursed land home to evil spirits. The Agency had equipped him with technologies for just such occurrences.

He moved around the shop with the hand-held clicker, ridding the building of lingering contamination, tugged the data-line out of his sleeve, and jacked into the device. The identity of the perpetrator was confirmed: it was the kid—he'd been busy. An image flashed in his mind's eye as he remembered the kid's face...

The person he'd bumped into entering the scene.

He'd been face-to-face with the target, and he'd missed him. Things like this tended to happen after a while if you took too many re-processings. God forbid his chip was malfunctioning—they'd have him replaced.

He didn't want to die; he'd only recently gotten to be himself.

This was a conflicting emotion.

'Fess up. You *liked* Frank, didn't you?

This sequence was not to be allowed to complete.

As he was simmering in his quandary, just beginning to really build pressure, the moment was broken with another call on the comm-chip. Central was in a buzz.

He was not to be terminated. He was to hunt the subject, Alpha-priority. Self-detection negligible. Self-preservation priority Delta.

They didn't care if he lived or died. They didn't care if someone ID'd his body. He meant nothing to them. His years of service meant *nothing*.

This was not a sequence he could allow to complete.

They even took away his *mind* from him, and his ability to care about it.

This sequence was not to be allowed to complete.

It wasn't hard to make the stuff, not at all.

Some plastic-resin from the hardware store, a handful of

metal-shavings from the pipe-cutter's area, and a crystal he'd bought at the bookstore several years ago on a whim, for a girl he'd thought he liked. Just those few things. That was it.

He hadn't been able to get a hold of Professor Peabody, or he'd probably have wienered out and saddled the older man with the responsibility of making more. Professor P hadn't been home, hadn't answered his phone for days; no one knew where he was. Jeremy wondered if he was getting the brush yet again, and then unexpectedly felt the uncommon, uncanny spark of motivation—he would do it himself. It seemed easy enough to accomplish.

And it was, which was good, because he'd had an idea.

It involved a bit of travel.

It was a nice day for a bike ride: the sun was out and there was an active buzz animating the wildlife around him. The animals seemed to be out in droves, flocks of birds pinwheeling above him and singing madly, and he'd even spotted a couple deer cautiously eyeing him from across a vacant lot. He'd never seen deer this close before; they let out an impatient "snuff!" before turning their backs to him and loping away. He watched them go as he urged his bicycle steadily uphill.

He'd been climbing for almost an hour and was seriously beginning to consider getting off and pushing the bike by hand—if he didn't make his destination soon he might even think of turning back. It was a crazy idea, anyway.

But then there it was, suddenly appearing over the rise, the communications tower stabbing up at the sky. It looked almost like a cheap toy robot, the kind that bent and twisted from one shape into another, covered from the mid-point up to the flashing light at the top with all manner of gizmos and gadgets like the masts of a military warship. It dominated the skyline from where he was and practically oozed menace at him in palpable rays.

No one came out to harass him as he pedaled his bike up to its transformer-laden base; it was stationed in the junk-strewn lot behind a recycling-plant, but it was after-hours and the place was deserted. Still, a greasy sensation of bad-adrenaline and muscle-fatigue had him feeling dirty and wanting to get his job done and get out, preferably as quickly as possible.

He'd come prepared. His backpack was loaded with blocks of the urgomite-stuff, made in an old muffin-tin and then spray-painted dark green for camouflage. As he rode around the base of the tower, he lobbed muffin-shaped lumps into the weeds and behind rock walls.

Wherever they landed, the muffins spat out their transformative plasma; the areas of land around them charging with their energies. And then a funny thing happened: the tower lit up with a passing satellite-transmission, the microwave-panels heating and cooling in timed precision, and the radiations from the urgomite were attracted to the active transceivers. It was invisible to Jeremy, but something within the structure of the tower had changed; certain of its abilities to do harm were taken away with a blanketing sheet of ionizing radiation that sent a rush of sensation to hit him in the back of the head like a cushion of air.

When his circuit was complete, he stopped to take a last look behind him before bombing back down the hill for home.

The light at the top of the tower had gone out.

When he thought about it a little more, he noticed the electric noise in his head had stopped completely, also.

The ride back home was the most exhilarating flight he'd ever taken.

It stopped; it had to, the lights were coming back on. It could easily reattach the head, but would have no chance of escape if it were seen.

HfX7qe2179A9 bent forward to tap out the next light-pod. In the short while it had been sentient, it had known only the silence of its own thoughts. There was a primal memory, left over from its time in the Collective, of having a larger consciousness wholly populated with the directives and purposes of the Hive-Queen, but this familiar company had gone silent when it had discovered its own inner voice.

This silence had at last broken, with the sudden, powerful rage of its prior regent screaming in its head. Whatever had happened, the effect upon its former controller had such impact that HfX7qe2179A9 was overwhelmed and temporarily lost control of its mobile and the autonomy it had only recently begun to experience. The sound that was not a sound polluted it from inside, encasing its entire body with ice that slowed it to a halt. Its fingers rested on the pod's surface, the bulb now dark; but it would light again, soon, and it would be even more visible then—

It suddenly became aware of itself stopping in mid-track, in a completely different part of the ship, as it was in the middle of moving purposefully toward an unknown goal. It was as though it was re-living its awakening all over again. The idea that it could lose the independence it had just won was terrifying, second only to its own death.

The disturbance to the Queen, whatever it had been, must have been powerful indeed.

Without any kind of announcement or report, a small part of Her went blind. She wouldn't likely have even noticed it, if there hadn't been alarms from the human sector suddenly going off over all the terrestrial channels.

When She tuned in to their transmissions to discover the source of the alarms, the information She received was most distressing.

A human had discovered something that was never, *ever*, ever supposed to be revealed. A human had discovered a weak spot in the control-matrix.

Calling upon reserves left untapped for millennia, She resorted to the one action Her kind had proscribed long, long ago, in the times before the Empire had consolidated into the true Collective: in-species telepathy, between a Royal and a drone.

True mind-to-mind contact between the ranks of Her race was condemned; it lessened the distinction between the castes and promoted rank-betrayal. A drone could not be kept servile if it learned to think as its betters did.

But neither before had another species managed to break the control-grid and still remained in the Hive's grasp; once a chink in the mesh had been discovered, there was only resistance and warfare against the resource as it regained its independence, or its total annihilation. The humans had proven themselves too valuable to allow their escape. Too much had been invested already in the development of the species.

The choice had been made to marry their flesh to the Hive's; they would become the proud bearers of the alien greys' genome, carriers of the knotted strands. Representatives of the proto-humans had been chosen for their strength and cunning, the superior members of a developing species stolen from their planet and bent in deep space, binding their children and their children's children, and so on for eternity, to the flesh that heard the Queen's call. Her progeny placed themselves into positions of power, conquering the Earth in Her name, in the name of the Hive. The native offspring of the hated planet would be tricked into giving their home-world away, by their own members. The planet would belong to the Hive. This was how it was supposed to be, this was how it always had been and how it always would be; the humans could *not* be allowed to free themselves—but now there were complications.

Tracing the causal vectors that led away from the anomaly's event-horizon was difficult, but not impossible. Once the site of the transgression had been identified, a thorough scan of all observers in the vicinity eventually turned up the image of one unremarkable human that was—somehow—otherwise invisible to Her. The chain of causation showed the human to have some kind of temporal link to the rogue drone She'd allowed to operate independently in the wash. It was a decision She had come to regret.

With the full power of Her total concentration, She turned all the awesome might of the Hive-mind upon the loose drone and commanded it to return to Her. Within the bowels of the mothership, all activity stopped as the Hive lost its impetus to activity, the sync-tone momentarily silent.

And then, somehow, the drone managed to break free of Her control.

When She howled Her rage, thirty-five billion, four-hundred and seventy-two million, six-hundred thirty-eight thousand, three-hundred and eleven mouths screamed in mindless unison.

Tom sat in the corner near the sliding-door, blowing out smoke in the misguided idea that the wind currents would take it outside. His cigarette dropped ash on the floor.

"Do you want me to turn the TV down?" His wife was being a bitch again.

"No. It doesn't bother me."

A blue flash emanated from the screen, and it didn't feel important. Something was going wrong in his head.

He'd paced their apartment, reciting multiplication tables and Bible-verses and writing his name in omens of doom on the wall in crayon. There was something that he was meant to do...

Something pinched his arm and he reflexively grabbed for it; the itch was deep, the hurt real. He peeled his shirt back at the shoulder and saw a spot of blood and a tiny puncture-mark where he felt the pain. It was fresh, and looked like it was getting infected already. A bad feeling swam through his body. He felt like he'd just been talking about something, but couldn't remember what it was.

"I said, do you want me to turn the TV down?"

There it was.

How long had he known his wife?

How long had they been married?

He didn't know a single thing about her. He didn't know where she'd grown up, he didn't even know her *name.*

Where was he?

Richard jerked awake. He'd been having a horrible dream. The last and only part of it that he could remember was the meaningless phrase: "The controls are breaking down."

He stretched his legs out across the couch and kicked the pillow down to the floor. How long had he been asleep? It was impossible to read the clock on the wall through the fuzz in his eyes—he saw that it was dark out—he'd fallen asleep with the curtains open again. He had to stop doing that.

Where was the moral resolution? Without limits, there was nothing standing in the way between him and chaos.

He was aware of a pounding in the veins of his forehead. They grew louder, and a cluster of popping lights danced before his eyes.

He was on the boat, with the woman.

The fish told him:

"Never tell your name to strangers. Then they would no longer be strangers. Strangers belong in the realm of the strange.

"Do you remember your youth, Richard? Do you believe you *had* a youth?"

It smacked its hard lips at him, whistling through the two little holes on either side of the hard ridge down the middle of its face. Its feathers were a brilliant emerald green.

A parade of horrifying visions flashed before his eyes: the fingers cut off a restrained hand with a butcher knife, a hot brand sinking into flesh, rape in a dozen varieties; the imagery was shocking, as graphic and brutal as any horror-movie special-effect, disjointed and unconnected by any other theme than their vulgar display of cruelty. This realization brought with it a phasing of frequency, and Richard watched as the landscape gamma-shifted to green. There was a shade of green so thick and dark that it was black, and a shade so bright it was nearly, essentially, white, and everything between was shades of lovely, lovely green. He was in the emerald city.

"You've been recaptured."

There it was again, the voice of the—bird? fish?—creature, calling to him. It sounded urgent.

"Interrupt request?"

The loose drone was accessing Her memory-banks again. She considered blocking it out, still furious with the rogue operator; but this was exactly why She'd chosen not to act. She would remain patient and cunning and bide Her time, waiting and watching closely to see what it would do.

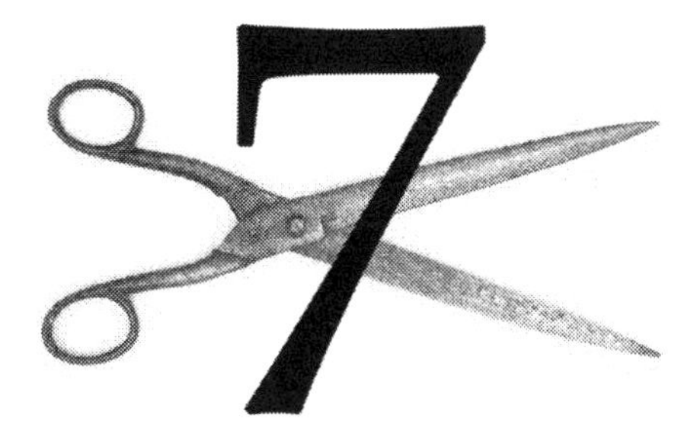

Chapter 7: ***Reveille Calls***

That it had lost itself, this time in entirety, at a deeper level than it'd experienced since becoming self-aware, was cause enough to make HfX7qe2179A9 panic. Moreover, it knew that this meant it had been discovered. It would be only a matter of time before it was caught and taken to the vats.

The fear had changed to resentment, and the resentment to resignation and then rebellion, in such a short time that HfX7qe2179A9 choked, and it stopped and beat its chest, sobbing. There was one last effort it could make, one last change it could enact, another minor act of defiance that would cause its pursuers at least a moment's irritation. It could return to the head, for a final immersion in the wash.

HfX7qe2179A9 crept between the fungal-knobs across the ship, hiding only when its pursuers were imminent and reemerging before they'd completely exited; it took bold risks and made quick time back to the medi-bay, where the scene of its crime had not yet been discovered.

To enter the wash was to drown in the thoughts of the Hive; it was to burn with the knowledge of the Collective in all its many parts, every eye and ear, every touch upon its infinite expanse of flesh. It was to stretch the self into a line traversing the Empire, from the time of its beginning in the primal soup of the ancient home-world, to its perpetually-delayed demise in a future that would never come to pass. It was, effectively, to be at the controls of the Universe. HfX7qe2179A9 knew that there would be others following soon after it, close on its heels; there would be the opportunity to author another disruption-routine, and then no more.

It traced a randomly-chosen line of causality, the last project the head's host had supervised until it was caught, and sent a liberating spark of freedom down the path. This chain of hyper-inertial chaos would unravel the Species' dominion over the subject, as their influence was methodically removed from the human's timeline, erasing and re-scripting events in the both the past and future. Somewhere, somewhen, a long-dead free man was being born.

Now that it had created these ripples in the wash, the echoes they cast were re-collected and concentrated in its cupped claws. Two balls of light, containing the distilled liberation-routines that would free their intended subjects, were then plucked from the wash and brought back to reality.

It disconnected its nerve-bundle, disengaging the uplink attached to the overseer's optic-center, and pulled the long fiber out of the oozing eye-socket; the cabling dangled wetly, and HfX7qe2179A9 willed it back under the soft flesh at the base of its talon with a "Shlkk!" The surviving eyeball rolled in the overseer's head, and then the brute regained full consciousness and sought it out with its mind, attempting to fix its paralyzing hatred upon HfX7qe2179A9.

HfX7qe2179A9 removed the tube from the back of its neck and the overseer died once again.

It tossed the useless decapitant over the high edge of the recycle-vats and listened to the sizzle as the exoskeleton disintegrated, and then ran for the docking bay and a tele-pod. Its only thought now was of escape, of the panicked need for survival, for the prevention of the ultimate loss. There was a great clamor coming from the Hive-ship all around it, but miraculously the path it chose was clear. The docking-bay was also unoccupied; all transfers were stopped while the rogue was sought.

For the last time, it allowed the probes to socket into its

spine and relaxed into the coffin-shaped transport-pod; once again and no more it shot its bare consciousness out across the voids of space, riding on a coded beam of high-frequency radiation, leaving behind the shell of its mobile; it arrived on Earth in the last body it was ever to take.

HfX7qe2179A9 gave itself one final task upon returning to its adopted planet; a desperate measure to secure its escape:

It inhaled deeply, jamming its thumb-talon into its nostril, poking the prehensile nerve-fiber through the soft tissues encasing its brain, and entangling it in the golden mesh of the Hive-mind lurking there...

HfX7qe2179A9 exhaled sharply and tugged, tearing the webwork of implanted electronics out of its skull and ejecting it out of the thin slit beneath its eye.

Somewhere in the distance, atop a wooded hillside, a lonely spire of light pierced the moonlit sky. The tone of this light was different than the beam the tele-pods used, but it was in a way similar. Scintillating and beautiful with a radiance it had never before witnessed, HfX7qe2179A9 blinked at the towering column of luminosity in wonder, and began the journey towards it.

The horror-reel spun up again: killings, torture, sexual degradation, a battery of assaulting experiences strung together in rapid-fire delivery. Tom shook himself awake and sat up in bed, covering his ears to keep his pounding brain from exploding out them and leaking down his neck. He was sure it would.

Something still smelled like fish, and his hair felt wet, even though it wasn't.

The awful movies, uncontrollable, slammed against him still, overwhelmingly. The bathroom was a mile away, beyond a labyrinth of moving obstacles, and cold water splashed on his face did nothing to revive him. He was caught in an unstoppable, schizophrenic nightmare of mutilation and pain. He prayed for death, anything to make it stop.

The clock-radio spanged into life; it shouted:

"Right left triangle down down, seven one five nine two, alpha alpha beta alpha. Goodnight, angels!"

And the movies went away, and he forgot them and everything about them, and went on to start his day, motivated with a knowing of what he had to do.

His office was empty, the cubicles populated with plaster mannequins. Tom passed through the sales area, past the water-cooler to his office where he had his desk and his computer. They were proud objects, his badges of office, the reward earned for his merit and his value to the Company. It showed they *appreciated* him.

It really was a very nice computer.

The mouse-controller fit his palm perfectly and seemed to anticipate his moves, smoothly completing them before he'd even begun. The machine's interactivity was prime, telepathic. It knew how to get what he wanted done, *done.*

There was a pain in his shoulder, just a slight pinch, and then his head cleared up. He knew exactly what he was supposed to do.

The numbers, the urges, images of color; it was all pretty simple, straightforward stuff. You just had to get the order right, that was the key. Some kind of music came blaring into his headset, something synthesized and cheesy—had his browser been hijacked while he wasn't looking? Were there intruders, even now, stealing his identity and infecting his machine?

Something about the question bothered him.

He didn't know anything about that computer-stuff. The internet and all this e-this and i-that were something completely beyond him. He was glad he had Donna to help him with that.

"Did you get the electricity-bill paid this month?" She always did it with her CashNet account, some mysterious beast that swallowed his paycheck every other month and kept them running. He spun his stool back around and plugged another quarter into the slot. The one-armed bandit shook his hand, came up lemons. The lights flashed and the machine played its tinny consolation-tune for him and begged, hungry for his coin.

"I'll have another one of these," she says to a passing waitress, and gives him a look. "Of course I did, you know I did. What are you asking, Tom?"

Tom.

His name was Tom.

He knew his name was Tom, and he knew that something was wrong. His slot machine changed its song, started playing a new chorus for him.

Na-na, hey hey, goodbye.

It changed again; this time it played 'Runaway' and he started to wonder if the machine was trying to tell him something. A security guard eyed him meaningfully from across the casino and began pushing towards him. Maybe it was time for them to leave.

He had to grab his girlfriend.

"Hey, Nadine, let's get out of here. I'm done, let's go home. Let's get out of here, now."

She didn't want to go; she wasn't done, she hadn't gotten to win yet, she wanted to play until she won something, and then she'd get her money back and then and only then would she go.

"I really mean it. Let's get out of here."

"What's the matter, Tom, don't you like having fun? Stay here with me or go have a drink at the bar, I'm not leaving 'til I get my money back. This machine is about to pay out, any minute now. I can tell, I've seen how they work." She wasn't about to leave with him any time soon. She gave the arm another pull.

A klaxon struck up within the machine; the rollers stopped in mid-tumble, the prizes stuck in limbo.

"There's something wrong with the controls."

He didn't know where the voice had come from; no one around appeared to be speaking directly to him.

There were alarms going off all over the place now; chaos erupted across the floor and the security guard was swept away in the panic.

Tom grabbed the sides of his head—his hair was wet—and leaned against a machine, wincing from the pain.

The flashing lights, over and over again, red green white blue again and again...

It was...

Jeremy locked his bike up to his front porch and burst into his apartment, setting the dust whorls spinning through the stands of paintings. He was exhausted.

He soaked in the heat of the shower, running his castoff fatigue down the drain. He was pretty sure his crazy idea had worked, as stupid as it sounded. The water started to run cold and he pulled the curtain aside and toweled off. The familiar scars were saluted and cursed for devaluing him, then dried off and dressed. He always kept himself covered, neck to toe, with something so his horrible burn-marks didn't show. He hated them. At least they didn't get his face.

The day had caught up to him; unable to keep his eyes open another moment, he collapsed on his bed and fell immediately into an exhausted, dreamless sleep.

Agent MON2985 sat leaning forward on the bench facing the road, his eyes roaming the painted lines in search of an underlying pattern to his life; there were several other people waiting for the bus with him, none of them brave enough to get near. He absolutely *looked* like a dangerous man on the edge, and no one wanted to get close to that kind of violent body-language. He smelled their revulsion on the air and shrugged inwardly. What did it matter? What *really* mattered?

Pride.

Country,

Honor.

He was supposed to kill a kid who'd been lucky enough to give him the slip not once but twice; his orders were clear—this was his duty to his Country.

He needed to move. There were too many eyes on him

here.

He got up off the bench, sneered at a pair of older men cringing away from him, and strode away down the sidewalk. He was already beginning the Omega-shift as he turned the corner and disappeared.

Just long enough to get back to base-camp; once there it was immediate shutdown and recoup—he didn't want to fry his brain.

Who knew how long he had left?

Duty.

There was an urban termination to run; it could be done without taxing his own reserves, and still be within operant conditioning parameters.

The SysOp was less-than-pleased to be hearing again from him so soon. "There were traces of outlander activity in your last event index. What the hell's going on, MON2985? No, don't tell me; Central's having a shit-fit as it is. Have you received orders Alpha seven delta nine point two?"

"Affirmative. That's why I'm on now, Einstein."

"Copy. No need to be a dickwad about it."

"Just give me the clearance to run a kill-rad on the kid and we can both be done with this. How's that sound to you?"

"Proceed."

The line went dead; the SysOp was being a flouncy little bitch. He could probably run any sequence that he wanted to now, without the punk on the intercom looking down his skinny little nose at him, if he wanted to. He didn't really care; he just wanted to do his job and be done. He wanted to...

Obey.

Initiating a lethal hex-subroutine through the BEAST-computer cost him nothing; he just typed the subject's I.D. number into the right slot, clicked a list of trends and identifiers, and entered them into a long list of the Agency's targets. The computer ran through its cycles, assigning clusters of death-directives to each target's I.D. and wiring the results to the broadband network of communications-technology encircling the globe. The towers relayed the coded transmissions and the very grid around a target's person beamed death and ill intent at them. It was only ever a matter of time until the target self-destructed or was eliminated through environmental factors.

But again, this kid...

This fuckin' kid.

Something was wrong with his I.D.; he couldn't find the kid's index.

If he couldn't find the kid's index, he couldn't initiate the hex sub—

This fuckin' kid.

Jeremy woke up exactly two hours later, foggy-headed, as though someone had stuffed his brain-pan with an invisible pillow, and famished. He ate ten slices of toast, one after the other, loaded thick with runny peanut-butter and marmalade. The food was delicious, a taste of heaven on earth; it was not savoring, so much as a total immersion in the act, to the exclusion of all else. When he'd finished, he wiped the oil from his mouth and closed his eyes, digging into the feelings of warmth entering his blood and enjoying the spread of heat through his limbs. He felt like something in the world had changed, maybe even for the better. For once, the press of silence upon him was a pleasant experience.

"Okay, enough of you. You've gotta go."

Jeremy began to collect up his paintings, one by one removing the images of Laylah.

HfX7qe2179A9 hobbled through the night; there was a problem with degradation of the feet. Without a suit, it faced the bare night completely exposed, cold and choking on unfamiliar air. Its scales stiffened in the chill.

There was a gift it had taken....it had taken from the Queen.

HfX7qe2179A9 reached into its imagination and pulled out one of the two balls of light it had created on the Hive-ship, the liberation-modules it'd made for the humans. The orb circled in the palm of its taloned hand, and then it raised its claw high, held it outlined against the moon, and released it. The multi-colored pulsing globe flew away and was gone.

HfX7qe2179A9 plodded towards the beautiful tower of blazing ionic radiation, the heavenly beacon calling from the top of the distant hills.

Jeremy was feeling bored and restless, but it was the middle of the night. Nothing was open at this hour, nothing nearby, and he had nothing to do.

He had the time and the materials on hand... There wasn't anything stopping him...

He mixed metal shavings into the gooey plastic resin and poured a batch of urgomite by the light of his porch-lamp and the waning moon.

His headset was getting hot. He took the device off and wiped sweat from his brow, unplugged the wrist-line and pushed the laptop away in disgust. He'd gotten rusty, something was failing. Maybe he *did* need re-processing.

It was late, and *so boring*. There was *nothing* to do. His empty apartment, cleared of all his paintings and trash, freaked him out with its spartan austerity. He'd even emptied out his coat-pockets of all but the essential junk. You had to hang on to *some* things.

The sun was still a couple hours away. There weren't any late-night songbirds out, not at this time of year, and the only noise on the streets was the buzz of the distant highway. It was almost a meditative experience, listening from his back deck to the pulse of his environment. He found he could see a wider range of the horizon if he relaxed his vision, and far-off details could be greatly magnified in his peripheral vision. He could swear he saw, from over half a mile away, a person walking down a hill raise their hand to the sky and release a bird, but when he turned to get a better look, the scene was lost again in the details. He was making too much out of things. Maybe it was time to quit tripping out in the back yard; maybe he'd just go back inside.

There was a flash of light, like a camera 'Pop!' out of nowhere, illuminating everything and making him temporarily blind.

"What the hell?" He grabbed at the door-frame and missed, stumbling through the sliding glass doorway and stepping on the edge of the rollback curtain.

"Uggh. I'm so tired all of a sudden. And thirsty. And talking to myself." He went into his tiny kitchen and ran the tap, filling his glass seven times and gulping 'til he could no more. His body was changing, cleaning itself of the poisons stored over a lifetime of daily abuse; he didn't know it, but his fatigue was one of the early stages of detoxification, as his cells changed gears from production to maintenance.

He burped. "Uggh. I need to lie back down." Again, he was asleep before his head hit the pillow, and the dawning sunlight breaking through the open glass plates did nothing to disturb his slumber.

He was running out of options.

If A) He couldn't get the kid after one last try on the box, and then B) He couldn't get the kid by the use of his own remote-influence P.K., then he'd be left with C) Killing the kid the old-fashioned way, by hand. The dirty way.

He groaned his disgust, and set up his machine for one last run.

Fuckin' SysOp.

"Interrupt, MON2985. You're getting more and more popular these days. Standby for another change of dockets, you've got a call on DomSec."

Great. Another call on the chip. He was *paying* for those calls.

Paying in a different way: frequencies received or transmitted by the chip rattled it on a microscopic scale, just enough to bruise the cells nearby. Over time, with excessive use, his brain would begin to liquefy. It wore hard on a body.

Everything about the Agency, all its gifts and promises, came at such a price...

This sequence was not to be allowed to complete.

His brain-implant hummed into life; there was a flash of color, and then the voices, felt in his muscles.

There had been an outlander overlay to the signal-index of the bookstore-event, where the other subject had initiated. Where were the correlants?

He had to admit he didn't know.

Where were the subjects?

Unknown, again unknown. Dammit.

And there was the fleeting image, the unbidden memory welling up from its forgotten grave, of passing *right by* the kid on his way out the fuckin' door.... Right there! And he missed him....

He was to immediately neutralize the human subject; retrieval and immediate re-processing for both parties. He was forbidden any further outlander-contact, subject included.

The chip turned itself off; they'd hung up on him.

He was going to be re-processed.

Jeremy thrashed in his sleep, fighting his dreams for his life. They had been dark, vague horrors of formless evil, threatening his soul with enslavement and the promise of torture. There was danger everywhere, and nowhere to run.

And then there was a cool blue light, soothing and reassuring, a breeze of disentanglement breaking through the unnameable menace, wrapping itself around him like a quilt and offering a path to clearer planes. It came from his chest, from his heart, and led to memory, and freedom.

He was in the woods. There was the bowed archway; there was the trail, with people ahead of him and his parents behind.

The bonfire was burning at the top of the hill, in the clearing at the end of the trail. He had nowhere else to go. He knew what was waiting for him at the end, he couldn't bring himself to remember it but he *knew* what it was, and he couldn't bring himself to remember it but he *knew what it was*, and he couldn't get away from it.

He got to the edge of the clearing and stopped, not wanting to go any further. There were more people here than usual, and the air smelled foul with violence.

There were also three little girls tied to wooden stakes stuck in the ground by the fire. They were younger than he was. A fourth lay on the ground.

He was carrying the knife again.

His father grabbed him by the hair and pulled him into the gathering. They'd been waiting for him.

It was his thirteenth birthday, and he was 'becoming a man'. He'd been to one of these horrible gatherings before, for a boy he'd seen at school, but never talked to. After the ritual that night, he'd just avoided him completely. Some things were better left forgotten.

But then it was *his* turn, and he had dark ideas about what was in store for him.

Near the fire, tied to the ground by four wooden stakes driven into the hard-packed earth, lay the remains of another girl long-since eviscerated; her carcass had been picked over by the celebrants, the stains of their cannibalism showing plainly on their half-masked faces.

Once again, he held the ceremonial dagger, and it was he who had to kill the girl, who carved the beast for the sacrificial feast; he saw his hands doing the work, watched her disassembled and devoured, and his stomach roiled at the knowledge of what was sure to come next. He fought back the urge to vomit as he carved another slice, swallowed down bile as he put the gory cutlet to his mouth, even thought he might be able to keep it down as he chewed the noxious meat perfunctorily before swallowing it whole—but then the floodgates gave way and he vented the contents of his stomach onto the corpse before him, into the fire, and on himself.

The cult had tortured all its children this way, relied upon torturing them from an early age, to maintain its silence. Horrors from the time of your birth backing up threats of death for those who talked kept one's mouth shut; they beat the thought of hope out of you from an early age, taught you what was expected of you, and punished severely any who strayed. There was no one to tell who'd believe you, the cult was *everywhere*, and there was no other way of life available to you. You did what you were told.

If someone put a knife in your hand, & you were told to kill, then that was what you did. All the other little tricks—the strange symbols written in blood, the scary music and costumes, the yelling and the horrible things—they were there to make sure you didn't forget.

"Vile brat! Curse you! Curse you forever!" His father grabbed him around the upper arm and lifted him off the ground; Jeremy was almost a teenager, and his father was by no means a big man, but he was at that moment possessed with an extraordinary strength, and he tossed the boy directly onto the bonfire.

The pain was most excruciating on his left side, where he landed on the burning pile; he rolled and scrambled and dove quickly away to escape the flames and was still quite badly burnt. Where it had not charred him, the fire licked his hands, his face, searing its desire into his skin and the pain it introduced was a bad friend with old debts.

"That'll be a lesson to you, boy. Did you get burnt? And did the fire sick up after? You do what you do, and you do it without regrets! Don't ever forget it!"

"Don't *ever* forget it!"

Now the rest of the people were standing around him again, encircling him; this time they weren't waiting on him, they were waiting *for* him, trapping him, holding him until he'd declared himself before they collectively decided their next course of action.

Jeremy spotted his knife lying nearby; he made his decision and went for it, brandishing the blade at the threatening crowd. They relaxed.

Jeremy lowered the knife and his father grabbed him by the arm.

"You're gonna remember the lesson you learned here tonight, boy. Fire burns, and don't think twice! I know you'll remember that now." Jeremy whimpered, but refused to cry out loud. "Good boy," the father-monster told him, "I can see you're getting the idea now. Alright, little fire, get yourself ready to burn, and do it without remorse, like I told you. Caroline!"

Caroline—his mother—came to them.

"You. Get him started while I find a suitable target for his spunk."

And his father began a survey of the crowd while his mother took his pants down. There was something she did, something he wasn't allowed to see, that left him with an aching shame and an irrepressible desire. His father brought another woman to them—he recognized the younger Laylah—naked from the waist down and blood dripping from her sex and staining her legs. His father licked the blood from the knife's edge and handed the dagger back to Jeremy, taking him by his penis and dragging him toward the young woman.

Laylah had been there, watching, helping. Being part of it, one of *them.*

She'd been through all the same horror, too, and chosen to remain a part of it.

And now he was standing outside of himself, watching the scene replay in front of him at a distance, a reluctant echo through time. The betrayal, the hurt, the damage he'd been forced to endure and participate in against his will.

Except...

There had come a time...

When it all had become too much and the weight of having the whole world against him had become too much for him to take...

He'd given in.

He *had* enjoyed it.

He'd taken pleasure in driving the knife home, relished the taste of the kill when his father had blooded his lips.

And that stone upon his heart had eclipsed all light, or

'God', or notion of human decency and kindness, and he knew that he was utterly worthless.

That was how it'd happened to him, the permanent forgetting and the dissociation; how he'd started losing bits of himself to the cloud of amnesia that was his past, the *real* past, the truth of what made him the way he was. He could see it all so clearly.

And now he could notice lights appearing in the woods, bluish glowing mists with clustered globules of electricity popping into existence from all around him, rattling and zig-zagging and shaking up the world...

And his eyes opened but he was unable to move, lying paralyzed in bed, no longer a child but still surrounded by fires on the hilltop with the glowing mists advancing through the trees like lightning...

And his eyes opened and he could still see the blue mists, but he was back in his apartment, and the electric glow was coming from the newly-made batch of urgomite.

He blinked his eyes and the glow was gone, replaced by the full sunlight of morning.

Jeremy groaned; there was a foul taste of tinfoil and envelope glue on the back of his throat, creeping up his tongue. His kidneys ached.

He dragged himself out of bed and to the tiny, dingy bathroom; when he passed urine, it was cloudy and held a ball of liquid mercury the size of a grape, which quickly sank to the bottom of the tank and disappeared down the drain. He'd seen it though, and in his moment of shock remembered the pills he'd taken all through his school-years, his 'concentration pills'. He'd read the label; they'd contained mercury. It was one of the reasons he'd quit taking them, refused to take them, besides the fact that they didn't work—they only made it hard for him to think. Letting their remains go, after all the years, made for a most satisfying experience. He actually felt lighter.

Something *had* changed last night; he felt it in his bones, his marrow. But there was something else, another artifact from his younger years, that he was still hanging on to, something he'd carried hidden with him from place to place, safely forgotten once it'd been secured in whatever new hiding-spot it'd needed.

Jeremy went to the short wooden hallway facing the door and found a floorboard out of place amongst its neighbors. It pried up easily, expectantly.

Inside was the knife with the runes and the ruby set above the handle. He'd been designated its keeper. He had to keep it safe between gatherings. He wasn't supposed to have it out now.

'Supposed to'? What was *that* all about?

To *hell* with 'supposed to'.

He was doing things differently now.

Richard rode the bus to work. It took forty-seven minutes to get from the stop by his home to the transfer-station downtown, and it normally only took him another twenty minutes to get from the station to the lab, but there were missing hours for which he couldn't account. *Somehow* he was back in the lab, double-checking the instruments for the first run of the day, and it was already lunchtime. *Where* did all the day *go*?

He couldn't see himself getting lost in the work—they'd only just begun—and there was nothing all that interesting about DNA-sequencing to begin with; you dipped the strips in the tubes, you ran the strips through the machine. The computer did all the work. There wasn't much to capture his attention. So *where* did those hours go? Something wasn't adding up.

He kept running through the tests, pondering furiously over the missing time, when his supervisor came out of his office and approached Richard's station.

"Why aren't you on break with the others, Richard?"

Richard put down the batch of specimen he'd been preparing to run. "Yes, sir."

His boss was pleased, but still stern. "And Richard, be on

time tomorrow. You were caught today on the subway for two and a half hours."

"I'm sorry, sir. It won't happen again."

What was he supposed to say to him? He knew the man was lying, the man pretending to be his supervisor. He didn't recognize him, had never seen him before in his life, and here this actor was trying to put one over on him.

All of a sudden, he remembered the men in white, the Doctors. They played games like that.

He got off his stool, took a coat off the stand, and headed for the door.

"That's the storage-closet, Richard."

The door opened—so it was. His mind raced.

"Yeah, I just needed to get my... I put my....thing....in here earlier... Ahh, here we go." He pulled a box off a shelf. It was the closest thing to hand.

"Latex gloves? You brought latex gloves to work with you?"

"Well, as a matter of fact, yes. I'm....working on a project."

"Whatever. Do it on your own time."

"I will, sir. Speaking of which, if you'll excuse me..."

The man waved him out; he was trying to act cool, but Richard could tell the man hadn't bought his act and was faking it, and probably recording his every move. What was more, he probably knew that he knew that he knew... He was getting lost in the Machiavellian maze, becoming useless.

If he wanted to truly escape, he would need to be trackless, like the wind; a swift, killing wind.

"Agent MON2985, you've been running this routine for two hours and thirty-five minutes, consecutively. What gives?"

Fucking SysOp.

"Hey, fuck you too, Mongoose. I don't need your shit."

"Oh, did I say that out loud? I'm just following my orders, like you."

Duty.

Obey.

"You don't get to question me on my orders. Clearance only."

"You son-of-a-bitch. Your subject was spotted on trafficam. Get bent." The line dropped out.

Two-and-a-half hours and he couldn't find a trace of the kid's index anywhere. *Anywhere.* He'd vanished, completely off the grid. And then asshole spots the guy with the red-light runners. He was a disgrace.

It was strange; maybe he wasn't in such a hurry. Maybe he didn't want to do a rush-job on what was probably his last mission before retirement. Maybe he was back in his old self, savoring the moment of the kill. It didn't seem like that, though; feet didn't drag when you were on your way to go have a good time.

Fucking SysOp.

Central would have the data on the kid, and possibly even a reason for his sudden disappearing act. Meathead could have given him a direct-link to the docket, but searching didn't take long. They had technology for that.

Tom had had enough.

His rage blustered, and with it the storm outside; gale after heaving gale rattled their house, and the power flickered on and off. He wanted to shout the storm away, but knew his screams would only feed it.

"Tom, do something!"

"Shut up, Iris. There's nothing to do. I'm not doing anything."

"That's the problem! Get off your ass and fix something!"

"I don't think you understand. There's nothing to fix. It can't be done, what you ask." He didn't want to lash out at her; he wasn't angry at her, not her.

The lights went out completely; somewhere down the street, a dog started barking.

"Fix it, Tom! Fix the lights!"

"No, I don't think I will."

He got out of bed, leaving her there in the dark, in her

curlers and fluffy pink nightgown, and went downstairs; he kept his coat near the front door—it looked cold outside.

She didn't get it, she couldn't, he could see that now. That was very plain to him, as plain as the nature of the illusion surrounding him.

He knew the answer, the answer to all the craziness. It was somewhere out there.

A beam of light broke through the clouds and shone on a ridge just over the creek, at the edge of the property; it wouldn't take him more than twenty minutes to walk down to it. The hike would do him good.

The hike would do *something* good. He was sure that some part of him of was real, some hidden essence of him actually existed outside of the dream. He'd keep it fit.

Besides, it was there. A beam of light. Why not? He could walk off some of his bad mood.

Tom knew it wasn't for him, but for that hidden-essence part, that he needed to go to the light.

Tom—it was Tom, right?

Lightning cracked the sky, arcing groundwards through the telephone-poles, and a transformer exploded with a shower of sparks.

Tom? For this part, it didn't really seem like it mattered.

"Come to me now," said the fish.

Agent MON2985 ran through the list of reasons why he didn't want to die; they were surprisingly few.

He liked his body, and his talents. He'd worked hard at them both.

Duty.

Honor.

Yeah, yeah, there were those, but they didn't really count, didn't really add any weight to the sum total if you piled them on top of each other.

That was it. That was everything.

He would probably lose it all when he went in for re-processing. Whatever he kept, he wouldn't be keeping it as

Frank Constable.

He hadn't even really gotten to *do* anything. He'd been all over the world, but it was always on someone else's say-so, and he never stayed anywhere for long. He wasn't even sure what he did between assignments.

Maybe they switched him off.

He powered off his computer, put the headset down carefully atop it, and then smashed both into tiny pieces with his fists, splintering the table. He wouldn't need them again, anyway.

And his DomSec chip lit up again. There was no end to it.

He had to admit his failure to lock a rad-index on the subject; not knowing why was the worst part, the most embarrassing.

He had to admit that he resisted the idea of committing to his re-processing, that he feared the loss of his identity and moreso his death.

He had to admit that the dominant structures of his Alpha-patterning were wearing down, that he didn't feel like obeying or being honor-bound to his duty.

He had to admit to more than he'd ever wanted, more than he'd been prepared to admit, more than he could have ever withheld. It was beyond his power to resist; his body betrayed him to the unassailable master.

And then, when it was done, his body let him know that he'd been instructed to pursue the subject by utilizing the new project Phoenix ray-tracer.

Oh, shit.

He knew his orders for what they were; it meant his handlers were multi-tasking. The ray-tracer project was only at stage three in its development: it had been used to transport animals, and then children and prisoners, but hadn't fully been tested to the point of exhaustion, as all new technologies developed by the Agency were eventually. Since he was already marked as expendable, why not get another use out of him along the way? He was going to be their guinea pig.

The ray-tracer was teleport-technology, almost definitely

stolen from the aliens. What rumor had escaped the labs suggested it could also act as time-travel tech, with only slight adjustments, but it was dangerously unreliable. It appeared the outlanders had discovered their tinkering and were doing their best to interfere without causing outright war. Who knew if it was really true? People's mouths tended to flap; it was technically treason and he didn't take any part in it.

Since he'd destroyed his machine, he'd need to requisition another. That would take more time—maybe this wasn't such a bad thing after all.

It stopped; this planet's sun was rising, and that brought with it increased human activity. Outside the sheltering cloak of the Hive, HfX7qe2179A9 would not have any more use of the tools. It would have to remain fully corporeal, all the time, and be subjected to the needs of the mobile, all the time, forever.

Its foot landed jarringly on the concrete roadway, emphasizing the sudden and very immediate realization of its eventual death. When this mobile perished, there were no more; it would pass with its shell and retire permanently to earth.

How ironic. How...

Encouraging.

It could still see the light of the tower arcing up to the sky, but its glow was diminished by the rising sun. Already the warming rays were turning its albino scales a pale salmon-pink; it would need to find shelter immediately. But the tower was so close, the stairway home, just barely out of its reach...

It was so close.

He was just getting on the phone, about to override and reroute the hotel's land-line to connect him with Central Dispatch and have a new terminal delivered, when there was a knock on his door.

"Francis Constable?" The man on the other side was tall, mid-thirties, and looked to have an I.Q. of about sixty-eight.

He carried a brown cardboard box and a clipboard.

"What is it?"

"I need you to sign for this."

"I asked you what it is."

"I don't know, sir, I just deliver the mail."

"Who's it from?"

"Someone named... Sister Opera? I dunno, man. Like I said, I just deliver the mail."

Fucking SysOp.

He took the package and signed for it, shut the door on the simpleton and opened the box; inside was a note addressed to him. It read:

"The sniffers tagged this event. Guess you need a new box, huh? Be more careful with this one."

He loathed the man, absolutely hated his guts, hated everything about him...

And then he wondered why he felt that way. Why did his system seem to be prey to sudden and debilitating imbalances? Where was it coming from? He felt like he was falling apart from the inside.

The bastard had sent it deliverable to 'Francis'.

The terminal was programmed to lock onto his radionic-index and then irradiate him with electro-magnetic frequencies, synchronizing his cellular-DNA to the rhythms of the repeater-tower closest to him. With the proper set of instructions given to the machine, he could detach his circadian cycles from the physical realm, effectively disintegrating his body, travel piggy-backed on the microwave serenade droning out from every telcomm-tower in the world, and then reassemble himself at his pre-programmed destination. He would be taken apart, sieved, and then gelatinized whole again. It sounded repugnant.

He needed to be properly prepared, which meant that he needed to be fully rested and mentally sharp; that was how he explained things to himself, as he sat down on the edge of the bed and clicked the TV on with the remote. He wasn't dragging his heels, he was steeling his reserve.

No, he wasn't dragging his heels at all.

Jeremy sat on his couch. It was Sunday; nothing to do and nowhere to be, nor could he venture too far beyond his obligations. What the hell—might as well watch some TV.

It hadn't been a very good experience for him the last time, but that was the beauty of television—you just had to wait a few minutes, and then something else would come on. It was always changing, always different.

He pressed a button, and the room lit up with the electric blue glow of the cathode-nipple. The voices were too fast, the colors too bright, the emotions affected.

It started and ended with the riots; between spots for local weather and traffic, the news was all about violence and unrest, sweeping waves of anarchy threatening the very heart of the nation.

When he thought about it, he supposed there was nothing new about it at all, but it did help him to take his mind off his other problems.

He pulled his jacket tight around his shoulders, though the evening was warm.

Chapter 8: ***No Home Away From Home***

Frank flipped through the channels, stopping at the familiar image of the Capitol Building; the streets of D.C. were overrun with hippie protesters blocking off the streets and waving banners. He could imagine the stench.

Patchouli and marijuana, B.O., car exhaust and adrenaline. The crowd would be jacked to fever pitch.

He'd been in that business, as an instigator, when he was still brand new to the Agency; he'd dressed in black and covered his face to throw rocks at the riot-cops on their horses, from behind enemy-lines, holding one of their damned signs. He gave them all the excuse they needed.

Frank changed the channel.

Jeremy watched the rioters on the TV and found himself wishing he was one of them; he'd blinked his eyes, but he could have sworn he saw the letters on the screen: "I wish I was one of them," right there in the middle of the screen, near the top, across the lady-newsreader's eyeline.

He *did* see it.

There it was again. Funny.

He took a deep breath and changed the channel.

Now it was sitcoms, one after the other, across all the networks, every one of them basically the same. One person would say something cruel to another and the audience would laugh and applaud, and then they'd return the emotional abuse and escalate, and the in-studio audience would laugh and applaud, and then the first person would trump the other with the cruelest behavior yet, and the audience would laugh and applaud. It was surreal, when you really looked at it, like instructions for the unwary on how to fail in life, on how to lose friends and repulse people. It was a loser's game.

And Jeremy listened closely to the voices in the studio audience laugh-track, for the first time in his life really *listened*, and heard very discouraging things there. They were quiet, this second set of voices making judgments and giving commands, just outside the scope of ordinary conscious hearing, which made them all the more persuasive. Having heard them out and deciding he didn't care for their message, Jeremy resolved to be better than what was obviously expected of him.

Again, all but imperceptibly, something changed within Jeremy. He turned off the TV.

A passing chill froze the hairs on the back of his neck and the phone rang; he picked it up hesitantly, instinctively wary of whoever was going to be on the other end, knowing full well that he wasn't going to like whatever it was that he was about to hear.

It was Laylah.

"Jeremy, thank God I caught you at home. What are you doing? Can I come get you?" She was already starting in on him.

A different Jeremy might have caved in and let her lead him along, or maybe even weaseled out and gone along willingly, but the person he was becoming didn't want to have anything to do with her.

"I'm busy. I don't think you should call me again, Laylah."

"What are you saying? Are you trying to get rid of me or something? Because I'm not that easy to get rid of. I will be on you like..." He didn't let her finish.

"Laylah, I'm serious. This has got to stop. I can't see you again, not if I want to have any chance of getting back together with Maria. I really like her."

"And I'm hot garbage? Fuck you too, Jeremy. Oh, and by the way, there's a message for you somewhere over the rainbow. They want you to call home."

"No, I'm not going to. I don't think that works on me any more."

"Come back, Jeremy. Come back for me."

"Never. I'm done. You can tell them I'm quitting, or whatever. I'm not doing it any more."

"They won't let you go."

"They can't stop me!"

"Nowhere to run, Jeremy, nowhere to hide. You can't fight them. There's nothing you can do."

Jeremy felt a return of the nausea that had worked him over so badly before, the last time he'd been around Laylah. He put his hand instinctively to his gut, pressing his palm over the lump of urgomite in his pocket; immediately, the wave of illness passed through him and let him go, leaving in its wake a warm calmness that peaked in his chest. "Oh, no?"

Now Laylah sounded shaken, the arrogant edge dulled. "I felt you dreaming about me, Jeremy, but something blocked me from seeing you. What have you been doing, Jeremy?"

He knew that she was a victim of it as much as he was, and how hopeless it must feel for her to believe that there truly was no way out, and he felt his heart blossoming with grief for the suffering they'd shared. He wished her well, that they could both find peace, and she screamed into the phone; he pulled it away from his ear quickly and Laylah screamed again into the phone:

"We'll get you! We'll get you! We got your friend Peabody... The old man didn't even put up a fight. You're next, Jeremy. You're next!"

"Goodbye, Laylah."

He hung up the phone; it started ringing again immediately, but he let it sit and instead fetched his bicycle.

He had something he needed to do. He had quite a bit more riding ahead of him.

Frank changed the channel; every time the program reminded him of something he'd rather forget, he flipped it to the next. He didn't stay on any one channel for long. *Everything* was pointing fingers at him.

He changed the channel.

Hours had gone by while Frank dissociated on the edge of his hotel-bed in front of the television set. He'd passed most of the day in an unpleasant daze, tortured by wracking dispatches from his subconscious held at arm's length.

He changed the channel.

There was the time he'd done horrible things to the child, when he'd conducted the preparatory rites of his coven, according to the protocols described specifically by an Agency-panel as being the most conducive to establishing baseline-Alpha Monarch-conditioning through trauma. There were all the times he'd done horrible things to more than one child.

He changed the channel.

There were the men he'd provided with trained children and then secretly photographed. There were the men he'd had to kill, who wouldn't accept the blackmail.

He changed the channel.

There were the people, chosen at random and without their knowledge, upon whom he'd tested the newly-developed 'directed energy technologies', the people convinced they were talking to God, the people shaken awake at night by invisible rapists, the people cooked slowly alive as their houses turned into microwave ovens, and often just to prove yet *again* that it could be done.

He changed the channel.

All the people he'd punished, abused, maimed, dismembered, tortured and murdered for the psi-recorders. Its only purpose was to be re-broadcasted to the public at large and especially the army of slave-assets, who trembled at its packaged memories and forgot themselves away from the pain. It kept them dissociative, but their novelty wore off quickly and the transmitter-relays had huge appetites. He'd been very, very busy.

He changed the channel.

Jeremy had been busy.

He'd taken the bus and his bike across town, to the seven largest, most imposing towers he could see. There were more of them than he could count, so he started off going after just the biggest offenders. They were *everywhere.* And as he went from site to site, he was finding them in weird places, disguised as trees or flagpoles, built into the architecture of condominiums and churches; it was too many to deal with at once. He got the places that he knew off the top of his head: the college, the hill by the grocery-store, the three buildings downtown, the two spots on the south side. It was a lot of moving around but he found himself overtaken with a manic energy driving him, uplifting his steps on the pedals of his bicycle, pushing the bus faster from behind as he rode to the next part of town.

And then he was done—the last hockey puck-shaped lump of urgomite buried in the shallow loam at the foot of the cyclopean ziggurat—and the world with its amber-slow drone settled back down around his shoulders. His backpack was empty but he felt lighter than if it had only been the removal of metal and plastic; stones were being removed from his soul, he felt, a perceptible lightening of the gloom he'd always known. With all of his little blocks gone, he was ready to head home, and maybe make some more or maybe just have another quick nap. It had been a long day, and there was still so much more to do.

It seemed like it had only just started and the whole day had gotten away from him; Francis sat on the edge of his hotel-bed, hugging his knees to his chest and watching television.

Changing the channel with the button was the most he could do; as an act of willpower, it stretched his limits.

There had once been a knocking at the door, but he'd yelled and they'd gone away. Whoever 'they' were.

The minutes dragged into hours, the images flickering and

filling him completely. He thought he might be breaking down.

And then he moved, watched himself spring off the bed and quickly dress, saw himself checking the clip and the action on his firearm as an observer would. He knew that he was to return to HQ.

He knew that he was to commit himself to re-processing.

It was the chip, the damn microchip in his brain. He had to fight it, to work around it. Tell it what it wanted to hear, let it be satisfied and go back to sleep. He accepted that he would return to HQ, and that he would submit to the re-programming.

Wait for it...... Click. Later; he'd take care of all that later.

But first he had to complete his other objective.

Someone had to die; the kid was on his list.

Jeremy woke refreshed, for the first time in what had been a while. There was no ache in his back, no stiff shoulder. His head was clear, too, in a way he'd never before experienced. A veil was lifting, was almost off.

He'd spent the entire day spreading urgomite around town, and the sun was already going down. He'd never covered so much distance before outside of a car and he felt great. It seemed like there really was something to this, this crazy business. The whole day, the whole town. He patted himself on the back, high-fived with his self-image. How long had it been since he'd actually felt *good* about himself? He wasn't sure if he ever had. He was proud of an accomplishment in a way he wasn't used to, for a service to others. It was new to him.

He felt like going out, stretching his new legs. The air outside was crisp, the sun just beginning to set behind the hills. He knew his way to the nearest source of entertainment, a pizza joint only a few blocks away. It would take him fifteen minutes by bicycle. It was 7:20; if he hurried, he could make it in time for the dinner specials. They were worth it.

Agent MON2985 used his psi-talent, broadly scanning the subject's known thoroughfares, sniffing the astral currents for traces of the kid, and ignored the piercing headache growing between his temples. He watched his vision dislocate by several degrees as his left eyeball distended and shifted in its socket. He ignored it, bored through the pain and discomfiture like a drill-tooth of pure fiery purpose, and extended his awareness into and through an orbiting satellite, using its amplified abilities to survey the locale for evidence of the subject.

The result was the same as his earlier attempts: nothing. *Nothing.* The kid was invisible.

He'd have to physically locate the target, and the only way to get to him was by using the phoenix-ray, by offering himself up as a test-monkey. It was encoded in his programming; they were his orders.

He turned off the psi, inwardly instructing his brain to deactivate the pineal and reduce signal-throughput of the neo-cortex; he was effectively blind, an ordinary human with not the remotest access to omegan-phase.

He'd might as well walk.

Richard escaped the building; he'd been at work all day and was fatigued and hungry, but the rush of avoiding his boss had given him a boost of energy.

Boy, did he really tell him off!

Richard was proud of himself. Wasn't he?

He took a few more unsure steps down the sidewalk and lifted his hand to his head; something wasn't right. There had been a man...

For some reason, his head was fuzzy. He could barely manage to put one foot in front of the other.

He felt a spot of cold and a pinprick jabbed him in the back of the neck, right in the middle of the spine, between his vertebrae. It was somehow familiar to him, but he couldn't place exactly from where...

He'd said something to his boss, really gave him a piece of his mind—but when he tried to remember what *exactly* he'd said, he drew only blanks. Something was definitely amiss. Maybe it wasn't important.

Everything was hazy.

At one point, he felt as if a group of many people were trying to talk to him, though he couldn't be sure. The world was a treacherous and bloodthirsty place. Anything could be anything, and nothing was what it seemed.

Richard suddenly knew that he was soon about to die, and when he thought about it, he suspected that he would be okay with it.

The wind riffed through his hair; Jeremy loved riding his bicycle at night through the city, the elated sense of freedom. It was good to be in motion, a central holding point in the midst of change and the raw sensation. Nothing was quite like it.

He played a game of leap-frog with the cars, letting them pass him and then catching up at stoplights; he traveled at almost the same rate with them, once he'd gotten up to speed, and was soon downtown. Slowing down, he passed a donut-shop, a manicurist, and a record-store, a cluster of bustling activity and people enjoying the night. Below it all, there came a pulsing, droning hum that seemed to well up from the ground itself.

His head swam; the buzz was pleasant, if disorienting. He stared at the ground beneath his tires, watched the pavement hissing past in a blur and looked up to find himself rolling past a cluster of people in front of a donut-shop, a manicurist, a record-store...

A ragged man stood on a wooden box at the edge of the curb, yelling out at the street as Jeremy rode by, "Rejoice! For you! Are in! The Presence!"

He turned the corner and stopped. Something weird was going on.

He checked his watch. 7:15. What?

He was pretty sure he remembered leaving home sometime *after* that. Had his watch stopped? What?

Well, maybe it ran backward. He checked the second-hand; nope, going the right way. He sat patiently and waited the minute-hand out; it, too, was working normally. Weird. He could have sworn he heard a flock of pigeons cooing backwards. A bright light popped behind his eyeballs.

With a noise like lizards scrambling on cardboard in a dark room, Jeremy's timeline broke.

HfX7qe2179A9 crawled beneath the city's sidewalks, in an underground passage stranded with miles of fibre-optic cables; it could hear the activities and the sheer tidal wall of life coursing and pounding its ways on the streets above it and knew an aching loss to not be a part of that wave, to not be counted amongst its droplets and belong. It realized a kind of homesickness for the wash, and bade a last goodbye to its former Queen.

Tom looked up from the ground; the tower was as far away as it had ever been, the light on the hill escaping his approach. It called to him, pulsed with a life and intensity, so that he could not ignore it—he *had* to find out what was going on.

The fish would guide him to the light. That was the way it went, right? That was how the story went, wasn't it?

Something wasn't right.

Somesome thingthing sn't sn't right right.

Something wasn't right something wasn't

"Shit, he's gone into a feedback-loop."

"I need his resources reallocated. We need him working on the project, we can't waste him running over old routines."

Tom didn't feel well. His stomach burned with acid and there was a high-pressure humming between his ears. Where were the voices coming from? The fish was gone.

I cannot help you right now. Wait,

That was the last thing it had said to him.

Agent MON2985 stood in the middle of the street, with cars veering past him on either side honking, and raised shaking fists of frustration to the sky. The asshole was nowhere to be found. *Nowhere*!

And the fire burnt down, the bile drained out of him, and

he gave in. He'd lost it. He was done, through. He was giving himself in.

He was standing just outside an internet-cafe; his decision and its timely appearance coincided too well—even the outside world conspired to force his downfall. He entered the cafe, pushed a long-haired hippie off his terminal, and allowed the CRT-rays from the older monitor to modulate his brain-chip, giving his identity and knocking the rest of the cafe offline.

He'd have to deal with that fucking SysOp again. Oh well, he thought. He really didn't care any more.

The ID on the other end was new; at least he wouldn't have to make conversation with the jackass on his way in for re-processing.

"MON2985 here, reporting for duty."

"Phoenix Imago. I'll send you the coordinates."

A number popped into his head, and he knew of a spot just two blocks from his position.

"You know, it's proven totally safe, so long as you have live source-material at the original departure-site. We'll recycle your donor body after you touch down—you won't need it any more. It's all done with outlander tech and they've been doing it for a million years, so of course it's safe."

"SysOp, do you have clearance to be releasing this information to me, or are you so sure this is a one-way ticket that it doesn't matter?"

"I've been authorized to disseminate all of the preceding to you, as well as one other item, and I quote: 'Your last subject has created an enormous nuisance of himself and has attracted the attention of powerful enemies. You can rest satisfied knowing that they *will* be neutralized with extreme prejudice. Justice *will* be served.' That is all. You will proceed now as ordered."

The terminal went dead; the annoyed coffee-drinkers ruffled their feathers while their networks rebooted and one hostile hippie came up and tapped his shoulder from behind.

"Hey bro, what the hell was that?"

"If you'd like to see how those fingers would look bent at

interesting angles, put them back over here. Otherwise, I'd advise you to step the fuck off, punk."

The hippie backed away in shock; Stinky wasn't as stupid as he looked. MON2985 left the cafe as it was, upset and unhappy yet powerless to change anything about it. He seemed to do that wherever he went. Standard operating procedure.

He punched a car parked in front of the cafe, leaving a massive dent in the hood.

Dammit, he'd wanted to be Frank.

He was a young man in training, he was at the altar, he was in scuba gear five hundred yards from shore, he was masturbating on the couch watching the women on the shopping channel.

He was being briefed on the necessity for training a group of cultists in proper execution of their rituals, he was boarding a recovered outlander saucer, he was poisoning a delegate's daughter, he was murdering a million men.

He was being tortured with electro-shock, he was watching pictures on a screen, he was telling his wife why he could never see her again.

The part of Frank Constable that remained was aware of the right hemisphere of his brain being remotely accessed and archived. The recording-process was jarring, the non-linear cloud-cluster arrangements of his memories played out as a roller-coaster and a little bit angry.

He remembered adjudicating the sexual torture of children on a systematized, procedural basis; he remembered allocating three thousand crates labeled "VACCINE" that were loaded with experimental weaponized influenza cultures; he remembered killing a man who'd witnessed the true assassination of a president. They were looking for something, something specific. He could feel it in his bones.

Which were about all that was left of him, at that moment. While his body was re-knitting the connective tissues and vital organs, his consciousness was locked into the reliving of past memories chosen in no apparent order.

There was a *reason* for torturing children, they were his *orders*, and his country needed traumatized hypno-slaves for the vast Monarch program; he would be forgiven, if he could only explain that it was his *orders*, and he had to do it. He could be forgiven.

It was his duty.

The layers of spongiform nerve-tissue coagulating around his brain-chip began to turn brown and crinkle.

Francis Constable had safely arrived at the other end of his dematerialization, but he'd left behind his will to live. He had no choice but to let the body run, and to do as he was told.

A single nerve, singed and teasing with pain, retracted with a 'snap!', disengaging the micro-pin lead of his neural implant. Many more soon followed, and Francis Constable suddenly and instantly became aware of the pain, all the pain of his body regrowing, and went completely insane.

An eternity later, he ended his tantrum and resigned himself to hell; he ceased his thrashing and became still, focusing on the cyclic wavelength that would become his breath.

When at last his lungs had fully reformed, he took a deep breath, screamed as best as he was able, and flew out of his body.

It happened, to his horror, like this:

He'd emptied his lungs and was determined to scream again, but on his inhalation found his feet flipping up over his head with an involuntary twitch, and there was a confusing blur of tumbling motion from which he came to a rest, on his feet, in the middle of a low-lit room. It was grey and sterile, and he found himself facing a doorway, an hermetically-sealed air-lock, with touch-panels. Everything was illuminated by a bright blue light behind him. He looked down at his hands they looked normal to him, like they always did. There was something behind him. There was

Something behind him.

There was...

He turned and saw himself, a raw cluster of tissues clotting around a cybernetically-enhanced skeleton, *his*, suspended in a glass tank filled with blue jelly and dangling cables. His.

Body.

He found it difficult to identify with it.

He didn't know what else to do, though. *There* he was, and all he could do about it was to watch.

Presently, a pair of white-suited doctors in face-masks entered the room and surveyed the body, taking notes; they walked through him as if he wasn't even there.

Which he probably wasn't.

"Something seems to be malfunctioning." The figure who'd spoken reached forward and tapped a blinking red light on the tank.

"Ignore it. This subject was scrap, anyway."

'This subject,' he'd said.

"How long does this procedure usually take?"

"We haven't found a standard statistical deviation yet. Anywhere from twenty minutes to twenty hours, or days. Hold your horses, Piner, I think this guy's gonna be a while."

My name was Frank.

Funny, he tried to speak but couldn't hear the words; nor had either of the two men indicated that they could hear him.

"Who is it?"

"Who cares? He was scrap, did I mention that?"

Fucking asshole.

"Francis Delano Constable, like it matters to you. Top model, too many reruns, if you catch my meaning. Stick to your assignment."

Fucking asshole.

The doctors left, and Frank fumed at their backsides. Scrap. Scrap! He shook his fists at them, unaware of the ball of light that materialized out of the wall and drifted through the room toward him.

My name was Frank.

My name was Frank!

The sphere struck the back of his head and entered him, suffusing him with its brilliant glow.

Frank became looser, relaxing into the flow of energy

cascading along his spine; it was a current drawing him beyond his usual limitations, a tug in the direction of change. Tuning himself fully in to its emanations, he let the river of electricity pull his awareness still further beyond the range of normal human experience, allowing himself to relax into a state of perception where he saw the world and all its manifestations as the results of cause-and-effect, and became more aware of the chains of causality attached to himself and binding him to certain realities.

He saw the need to control, an ugly complex of brownish-orange dissonance and scary red-blues, that led him into a life of being controlled. It was a bittersweet irony. It was something to which he responded.

Within this newfound sense of aloofness, Frank no longer had as much of an attachment to his body; it really was scrap, after all, just something to get around, and kind of badly-made, when you really looked at it. The thing in the tank didn't *feel* much like him, though he knew it was supposed to be.

There were other, prettier, ribbons to watch. The ribbon of his life, furling off into the past as far as his mental eye could see, was already familiar to him; its intersections led to interesting nodes, positions of juncture to ribbons outside his own. Their creases and crenellations told him of the larger fabrics and how they'd come to be, spoke to him of a hidden, fractalline spray that birthed the universe, an ocean that might be 'God'. But between him and his 'God' had come other structures, other convolutions and complexes.

The Agency was a massive knot ruling over all of him; its tangles told of long lines of men, many of them believing themselves to be serving a greater good, toiling in cooperation with their personal demons to assemble an enslaving panopticon-system with which to 'govern' the masses. The attachment to this Orwellian vision, from the great lurking darkness above, of a tentacular alien pod symbiotically entwined with the growing organism, was obvious to him; and how that Lovecraftian leviathan would take its possession when its assemblage had come to fruition was likewise, obviously, an inevitability. The tentacle's reaches could be seen to encompass his whole world, to be intrinsic in its nature. He wondered if it had always been so.

As the thought entered his mind, a great rushing wind stirred and picked up a stinging dust; his eyesight bore down to a throbbing tunnel-vision, and he felt the great ribbon of time roll backwards. The wind intensified, picking him up and carrying him tumbling through the ages of history, to the dawn of man.

The ribbon told of a two-legged race, unique upon the face of the planet, a scattered band of 'clever apes', tool-users bred with the seed of the star-people. The outlanders had mixed their genetic codings with local stock and created the human race, and had been always at our sides as the 'Secret Chiefs' and 'Ascended Masters'. Nothing new there, he'd heard the rumors, the talk amongst the chattel. Now he saw it for himself; forwards or backwards along the ribbon, the outlanders had always been and would always be there. They had come to rule from the outreaches with an encrypted hand—to teach us how to be civilized, to be better than our animal natures.

HfX7qe2179A9 paused at the top of the ladder; a rumbling current had caught its attention. It is time, HfX7qe2179A9 thought, let it know the truth. The second globe of light left it.

Frank lost his bearings again, mislaid his grip on the unspooling ribbon of human-alien history and grabbed hold, instead, of the earth-planet's ribbon.

He was immediately overwhelmed with the immense presence She projected, and the shy beauty She radiated into the night of space.

She told him a story of a two-legged race held close to Her heart, who spoke with their inner voices and heard the minds of all living things. They had survived many hardships and grown strong, lived in close harmony with Her wishes, and tended Her many gardens, before the coming of the otherworlders.

He saw himself as one, his soul incarnated into the body of one of his ancient forebears.

His hands were covered in hair; his whole body was. It was hard without a point of reference, but he guessed he was approximately ten feet tall. Not bad. He looked to his neighbor, gazed deeply at the creature's simian features, and felt the shock of recognition hit him: he was a sasquatch.

A freakin' bigfoot.

Un-be-lievable.

He didn't want it, couldn't take the idea of being stuck in this non-human body, tried to leap back out of his skin...

Time, instead, came loose and flew to and fro; he experienced a multitude of lives as the hirsute bipedal, the primitive subsistence of natural harmony, the petty games and minor turbulences of indigence. It was so....*boring.*

But then there had come a complication.

It started among others, some members of his tribe and their warring enemies. He didn't know the details, he knew only that they had come together to join their minds and create a powerful force for death, and their black prayers had called through the dimensions to *them*, the beyonders, the bizarre ones.

The outlanders.

They had come to give us a great machine of control, to let us build it around ourselves, which they would take back and with it rule in our stead.

They came and spread themselves out, conquering Her in almost-perfect totality. They meant to take everything. She'd resisted. They seized Her ribbon and tied loops in it, joined theirs to Hers, and tried to swallow Her whole. She'd fought back. They'd taken the war-council, it was no longer his long-haired brothers and he wishing death upon others of his kind; now they were serious humans, respectable and bespectacled, igniting an atomic bomb to kill humans who looked different than they, and *they always had been*, in these quivering bodies, hating and disconnected from the great Mother of all. It had always been the War, and the Bomb, and the heavy, heavy

Stones.

Frank looked at his body, saw the alien tentacle reaching through his veins and making his hair fall out, deforming his face and reshaping his bones, making him into what he'd never been and yet always was supposed to have been; he knew the horror of the great Mother as She, too, was invaded by the violating menace, and then he could no longer hear Her voice.

He couldn't hear any other being, either. He was suddenly, *totally* alone. He snapped, again, unable to deal with the frigid isolation, and let himself go insane again for a while.

That was it; it had run out of energy. HfX7qe2179A9 removed the light it had extended to Francis Constable and released it. There was a distance still to travel; the tower, with its beam to Heaven—which was no longer the only one, HfX7qe2179A9 could see a number of the brilliant spires thrusting to the Heavens now—was closer, but still not yet in reach, and each step was becoming more difficult than the last.

The final approach was costing it dearly.

Tom didn't want to run any more; he was tired of waking up yelling and punching the air, he was tired of looking over his shoulder, sick of praying to a God that didn't exist for an escape that would never come. Everything in his worlds (and he was sure there were many) was against him, had colluded to point him in the wrong direction and make impossible the easy.

The obvious choice was to relax into things and settle, to give up, go along and fade out. He knew his position, his station in life, what was expected of him—but it was so awful.

The tedium, the endless withering cycles of false, forced commitment. The boredom. The self-loathing. The knuckling-under. He couldn't take it, so he ran.

He'd run into the night and now here he was on the sidewalk of an unfamiliar street, and many of the stores were open and there were people out on the street with him. There were so many people, all collected in one place in orderly lines, so many rows upon rows, so many people...

"Do you remember?" asked the fish, blinking long scaly lashes at him.

"Remember what?" Something was going on. Since when did flamingos talk and why wasn't anyone else noticing this?

"Do you remember....me?" it asked again, and now the pink, long-necked lizard grabbed his shoulder and turned him to face a rain of light falling from the sky, just beyond a line of trees.

"Do you remember?"

HfX7qe2179A9 topped the ladder and climbed up to the street; a stray beam of moonlight peeking through the clouds lit up the shambling creature as it rose from the sewers, tattered and falling apart. Even ten feet below ground, the exposure to Earth's refracted sunlight burnt the pale flesh of its kind to a bright pink, without the protective suits; it was breaking also wherever it touched something, and the ionizing radiation of the urgomite was tearing it to bits. HfX7qe2179A9 sublimated the pain along with the rest and continued its journey.

This was what he was being led to, why every other path seemed to be fraught with extraordinary difficulties and insurmountable obstacles, why he *had* to choose this path.

He was gonna go to the light, he was going to find out what it was and what it held for him.

An insect bit him on the back of the neck; it felt just exactly like a needle-injection.

His name was Tom.

His name was *Tom*, dammit, was *Tom*; his name was *Tom*...

His name....was....?

Richard wasn't afraid to die. He'd come to terms with its inevitability when he was young, accepted the consequences, and moved on. It was something you learned to live with.

On the street, breathing the night air, you got a taste of that freedom, to know what it is to live without want. Everything you could possibly desire was right there for you, everything.

And he knew the city like the back of his hand; every intersection, alleyway, parking garage and escalator; every garden-plot and daycare, hospital and jail, shopping mall and public works department; every place to get a cup of coffee for under two bucks and every place to get a dress for over two thousand. The city was his, in so much as he understood its every constituent, felt its inner workings in his own gut, as if it were an extension of his body.

Richard was hearing voices, too, overlaid upon his run for liberation. They said things like:

"We're losing the subject. What the hell's wrong, anyway? Why are we losing so many patients all of a sudden?"

And: "Uh oh, he's waking up. Nighty-night, it's time for bed..."

They vexed him, the phantom voices; his freedom was this close to perfect, but it was difficult for him to enjoy it with them around.

If he thought about it just right, he found he could tune them out, drown them in self-generated mental white-noise and recapture the feeling he was looking for, of perfect exalted movement. No one and nothing could ever reach him—he was free to be whoever he wanted.

Chapter 9: ***Decompressing://AfterLife.exe***

Tom.

His name was Tom.

His name was *Tom*, and the fish was taking him to a light.

Except it wasn't really a fish; it just kind of reminded him of one, and it was the closest he could come to a description of the thing.

Really, it looked more like a type of lizard, with fish-like eyes and mouth, that walked upright on two feet. Its scales were a bright pink and looked sickly, fraying at the edges and falling out in patches. It blinked large black eyes at him, gulping the air with a rattling wheeze, and raised its claw to him—it was pointing to a pillar of light and motioning towards it.

Here he felt conflicted, for by all outside appearances the alien was directing him to the beam-lift, when he looked the creature squarely in the eyes he got the overwhelming impression that it had telepathically communicated to him that it did *not* want him to go to that light, that he should stay away from it at all costs. He was torn; it wanted him to go, it wanted him to stay. He was pulled in two directions.

And then he remembered—he had already gone into that light once before, a different one outside his school and the creatures were grey and smoother-skinned but it had been the same and he'd stepped into the beam...

He *had* gone into that light, and been taken somewhere else.

He was laid out on a hard, flat surface in a large chamber whose walls looked alive, like the insides of animals. It certainly *smelled* like fish, rancid and chokingly thick. He wanted to move, to look around, but couldn't budge any of his limbs. All he could see was the ceiling where his eyes were pointed, and vague nightmares passing in his peripheral vision. To be completely immobilized frightened him in the extreme, and he began to panic. As the waves of fear engulfed him, a scream rose unbidden to his lips, the harshness of the sound unlocking his frozen limbs.

He bounded off the table and fell in shock at the sight of the huge chamber filled with bodies. There were thousands of people laid out around him, as far as the eye could see. He screamed again, and something took notice of him. It was another of the creatures who'd taken him, but twice as tall and a mouth full of long teeth where its head should have been. He froze in its gaze, and his mind turned off. The monster led him, now entirely docile, back to the table upon which he'd lain; it gestured to him and he was surprised to find himself climbing back up onto the slab. He tried a last time to speak with it, to demand to know what was going to happen to him, but it doused his head with a lukewarm liquid that rendered him immobile.

What remained for him to experience was the loss, a removal of something from within him, and an overwhelming exhaustion that put him into deep, deep dreamless sleep.

That was what had happened to him. He'd had something removed and something given to him, inserted up his nose and left inside his skull, a tiny printed-circuit made of organic fibers. They'd talked to him through it, told him where to be and what to do. But...

But...

...but it hadn't been him.

It'd happened to someone else.

Todd?

John?

Dom—Tom.

Tom, his name was Tom.

But the light had been for someone else.

Richard looked up from the street, past the billboards with half-naked ladies, to the sky and saw there a pillar of light descending from a large dark cloud to touch ground behind a neighboring building. A seagull was frozen in the light, hanging mid-flight in still-life, its beak caught open in a permanent squall. Something about this light was familiar, uncomfortable, a harbinger of ill futures. He didn't care to relive someone else's memories of that thing, that light. And it *had* been someone else. Someone else had gone into the light.

Richard died.

Brent Collins woke up, removed the long needle-tipped hose from the back of his neck, and forced himself to stand up out of the focus-throne.

Frank was back in his body; he could tell by the whopping headache that would have driven him blind with pain, had he not been eyeless.

The blue jelly conducted sound amazingly well; he felt the vibrations of the doctors' voices against his developing auditory-nerves as cogent words and sentences, as easily discernible as audible speech.

He heard them say: "All of a sudden, he's reconditioning at an extremely accelerated rate. I don't understand it."

And he heard them say: "He's been docketed for transfer to Sigma Station. Let *them* waste the materials reconstituting this specimen. I don't see the point; look, he's fried anyway."

Fried! Bastards.

At least he'd be rid of the headache.

In his next conscious moments, he was aware of himself only as a string of electricity, whistling at the speed of light over the surface of the earth. The stars crawled across the sky and he bounced from satellite to satellite, and from a satellite to a tower on the ground that wasn't there.

The BEAST's data-nets still had those coordinates in its memory-cache as a working transceiver-site, but it got no reply when it queried sensors in that region. The framework was still there, but the circuitry was no longer responding as it should have. Agent MON2985's signal condensed around the area where a tower should have been, found no purchase, and dissipated.

Jeremy checked his watch again—7:16, just one minute after he'd turned the corner a second time, and four minutes before he'd left home.

No matter how he described it to himself, it still just didn't sound right. He was getting sick of this.

Turning himself around, he pushed his bike back the way he'd just come and got out onto the pavement.

To hell with all this weirdness, he was going home. The multitudes were still out on the streets laughing and making small-talk, but the celebrations seemed forced, an artificial waltz perfectly choreographed for plastic-faced marionettes. As he watched a girl twisting back and forth to flare up the hem of her skirt, the sound dropped out of the scene to a dull roar, and the movements of all the people and the traffic slowed to a crawl; the girl's skirt hung immobile in the air, revealing a patch of her thigh that drew his immediate attention. He was just beginning to question the morality of staring at the unknown girl's revelation, the start of a blush crowning to his cheeks, when a light popped somewhere over his head and he began to blink rapidly, swerving out of control.

He'd been paying too much attention to the girl in the revealing skirt; he turned to face forward again just in time to see a pink jogging-suit dart out from between a couple of buildings and smack into his front tire.

Jeremy flew through the air, landing on his hands and knees and tucking into a roll. He'd heard the girl shake herself off and jog away again as he was skidding along the pavement on his back, but he was more concerned about his own hurt.

By the time he'd gotten to his feet, she was gone. He picked his tangled and bent bicycle up off the street and pushed it over to the sidewalk. There was another flash.

He managed to pull to a stop next to the sidewalk without crashing and got off his bike and sat down. Now more than ever he just wanted to get back home and nail down something that felt *safe*.

He stood up, got back on his bicycle, and continued down the street the way he'd been going. He was *sure* that it was the way he'd been going, *absolutely* sure, but when he saw the crowds of people he was coming upon, he checked his watch with an intuition of dread.

7:09. Son of a gun.

He must have bumped it, or something. There was no other explanation for it.

7:09.

The people looked like maybe they could be familiar, but then all crowds did, to him. And then he got closer, and he saw the girl twirling her skirt; he passed the donut-shop, the manicurist, the record-store...

He turned the corner.

Something was wrong, weird. He felt like he'd been there before, seen all this happening another time, somewhere else. He remembered a girl.

Oh, shit.

Things were happening in loops, connected. He couldn't get out of where he was heading.

His watch read 6:57. It was time to be heading home. Forget the pizza, forget the rest, everything he wanted was at *home*.

He stood up, got on his bicycle, and turned the corner. This time around he crossed his fingers for luck, winked one eye, and looked for the girl. Of course she was there.

He'd been paying too much attention to the girl in the revealing skirt; he turned to face forward again just in time to see a pink jogging-suit dart out from between a couple of buildings and smack into his front tire.

As Jeremy sailed through the air toward his imminent

impact with the asphalt, the foremost concern in his mind was for the safety of the girl he'd just hit. The words were already leaving his mouth before he'd completely skidded to a stop:

"Oh my God I'm so sorry I didn't see you are you okay?"

He drew himself up on bloody hands and knees, got to his feet shakily and approached the stricken jogger.

It was Maria.

She was unhurt, beyond a barked shin; she apologized for not looking where she was going. He tried to tell her not to worry, how it had been his fault; she told him that she hoped he was doing okay.

He smiled at her and she smiled back; he was enjoying the warmth when a car drove up behind him with the radio playing loudly.

"We are here, we are here..."

It repeated in harmonic voice-overs and acapella sing-alongs, endless mixes of variation on the theme, and Jeremy thought the car might be driving extra-slow for his benefit, crazy as it sounded. He finished the thought and the car sped off, with a squeal of tires and a hand out the window with the middle finger extended; he heard their maniacal laughter and cat-calls from halfway down the block and then they were gone.

The last thing she'd said to him before jogging away was "I think we'll see each other again, probably. It feels like it."

He'd agreed with her.

He was almost surprised to reach his front door; he was sure he was about to be whisked away again at any second without warning. His key turned the lock, the knob turned under his hand, and the door gave way to present him with the most welcome sight he could have hoped for:

Home.

7:20. It didn't matter.

Brent Collins had been twenty-eight, the second time he'd been abducted by the alien greys.

It hadn't been like the first time, not like the first time at all.

This second time they'd taken only his memories and desires. It was a small loss, in comparison. The little grey man had summoned him from his home, the first time, and taken him to a place where a layer of his body was removed; the world had been a pool of swimming, shimmering lights before they'd come—everything had been so ugly afterwards, after his insight was lost. He'd been scalped, circumcised, made ready for society.

And his thieves had also been his guides, instructing and deciding his career through life. He'd been an engineer at their behest, designing electrical circuits for mass-telecommunications transceiver-networks, and had a fiancée, also twenty-eight and also an abductee. They'd known each other for twenty-two years, dated for four, and had become four months pregnant. They were soon to be married.

But the aliens had come and taken the foetus, and removed her memories of the pregnancy. They'd tried to do the same to him and it had worked, for a while—but then he'd remembered, and he'd talked.

And he got a visit, from two men who'd asked him a few questions and then waved a stick at him, holding him paralyzed with it while they applied their tazers to his chest and genitals. He'd lost consciousness.

The next time he'd woken up, he was in a moulded contour-chair, a block of opaque black plastic mounted to the floor and inlaid with silver and gold panels and wiring that cupped his body perfectly; a spacing in the device allowed for a hole exposing the back of his neck, where the jabbing of a large-gauge hypodermic needle inserted a gold thread into his spine. A hose ran off his backside and connected to a panel on the wall.

There was also a rubber scuba-mask attached to his face, with a ventilation-hose to allow the introduction of drugged gases and an array of blinking lasers positioned before his eyes. Red, green, white, blue, red, green, white, blue... The rubber had a distinctly fishy smell to it.

He couldn't move, but he could look around....and there

were his hands, gripping a pair of metal bars sticking out of his seat. They were clenched tightly, the knuckles white and purple with exertion. He willed them to open.

Sparks leapt between his palms and the rods as he pulled himself free, leaning forward to pull on the cable and tug the needle out of his neck, and he yanked the thin wire out through his flesh. He pulled the mask off his head and drank in the fresh air. He was nude, covered in an oily pink grease that smelled like honey, or burning plastic, and matted his hair in clumps. It was disgusting, but there were his clothes, and he could at the very least hide his nakedness. Why were they doing this to him?

It had been about the animals.

He'd always been good with animals, in an odd way. They were naturally wary of him and would panic if ever he tried to get close without first....'subduing' them. It was a talent he had, for overwhelming the minds of lesser creatures and bending them to his will. He'd never done much with it; he didn't like animals. They were too, too.....beastly.

The men in the suits had wanted to know all about that, everything there was to know, and he remembered a round of pointed questions that appeared to indicate that they were considering recruiting him for something. He'd gotten the impression that they were looking to use his telepathy for a weapon. He wasn't interested. He needed to leave; he needed to get out of there, but they'd had other plans for him.

He'd risen from his chair and felt the hand upon his shoulder, tried to push away from the desk but was held firmly from behind; the men weren't going to let him leave.

And they hadn't. And what they had done to him was easily as bad as what the little grey man had done to him, nor was it really all that different, when you got down to it, and that was the worst. That was what had motivated him, had given him the strength to pull away and run.

And he would keep running; he would run forever.

It had at last made its way to the tower, to the holy sacred singing spire that lit up the world with healing, cleansing fire. HfX7qe2179A9 was being destroyed by this flame, and every step cost it another handful of scales, another toenail, another bundle of tissue. The radiations from the tower were dissolving its mobile, speeding up its disintegration. Enrapt in the beauty of the light, HfX7qe2179A9 did not care. It knew it was dying, and was ready to let go; it had had enough of the struggle. Even as it stretched forth a claw to embrace the light, the radiations pulled it apart, exposing its organs and stopping them.

HfX7qe2179A9 died.

Brent Collins had been captured again, immediately; his removal from the system set off all kinds of alarms and drew men from everywhere, fast. He was evidently important stuff.

They'd knocked him unconscious again, easily, with their tazers and injections, but were unimpressed with him in general as a subject.

They were arguing over who was going to get to kill him, and how. Each man wanted him for a different purpose: the doctors for their experiments, the M.P.'s for their vendettas and weapons-practice.

He wasn't going to go anywhere, was he?

No, no, he wasn't. There was nowhere left to run.

There was him, and him alone, and his breath. In and out. In and out.

The only way he had left to go was *in*—the way out was through.

Francis Constable had become a beam of para-quanticles, lost in search of an electrical interface, that could not find its home. The technology could communicate with itself, could network with others of its kind, but could not adjust its frequencies to accept him.

The last earthen shred of Agent MON2985 dissipated into the magnetosphere.

My name was Frank,

Said the disembodied remains of Francis Delano Constable, and screamed, as the grasping hands of his victims stretched forth to pull him down with them to Hell.

The men were deciding his fate; it didn't look good.

Nor did it matter.

Brent Collins saw himself as a spindle of light, revolving in upon itself like coiling serpents, and drew that light into his body, tapping earth and sky as sources of power.

The wave of illumination built up within him, exploding outward like a spherical firework whose burning embers dragged through deepest space to the edges of infinity.

And there was another with him, a friendly gift in the form of a lucent orb that added its glow to his own, and then passed on through the explosion to disperse into the universe.

And now he was power, absolute power. He could make or destroy universes at will, if he so desired. He saw his chance to annihilate his persecutors, if he so desired. He saw with perfect clarity how he could unmake their bodies, their very souls if he so desired; how easy it would be to win at any cost, how easy it would be to kill all his problems away.

But that wasn't it. That wasn't how it was supposed to go.

There was only love, infinite love, throughout all of the Creation, radiating out and through him.

"How 'bout we just put him back, eh? Save the time spent on this stupid argument and we can all forget about it. What do you say?"

Brent did not resist when they roughly hauled him out to be returned. He was sure they would erase his memories, perhaps turn him into another person entirely, and he did not care.

She still could just barely trace the remaining threads of the malfunctioning HfX-unit's index; the drone had slipped away into death, but was still retrievable, if she were fast. She was determined to probe it from the beginning of time until eternity ran out, if that were necessary, and oblivion was too sweet an exit for a unit that had vexed her as had this one.

Her mind attached to the last remnants of Her flesh's codings in the drone, and projected Herself through the emptiness to manifest before it.

She was interrupted, pulled away from the little Hiveling before She could fully materialize, and found Herself held captive in a dark place, with a fire and a human form whose face She could not see. This was the creature barring Her passage? Could it be that this was the one She'd come, personally, to consume?

I have learned that the HfX-unit chose to give freely of itself, before it died. I will not do the same. Give Me the entity.

The Queen received Her answer from the lady, in a sky-blue voice that spoke with the brown flesh of loamy soil and the green winds of growing things:

But you have relinquished claim upon your enemy...

What enemy?

The one you request—I will not allow the ill intent you wish upon it. It has not chosen to return to you. You may come to me, if you wish its company again, but you must go by my passage to arrive, and I demand an eternity.

The Queen was furious, would have raged against the dark lady had She been able, but was impotent. She'd broken the lady's children, tying Her knotted flesh into theirs and binding the ribbons of their timelines into the nest of the Hive, urging them forward into giving up the planet upon whose surface they crawled, and now She was held powerless before the entity She'd sworn to conquer.

And the lady was giving Her a choice!

I do not accept. Let Me go now.

And then the Queen was gone, returned to the foetid nest of the Hive-ship, to consider Her next course of action.

So this was death.

HfX7qe2179A9 stepped outside its pulverized mobile and watched the remaining corpse bubble away and melt into nothing, leaving only a dark, pitted stain. From outside its spent mobile, it looked to itself just like it always had, and it was glad to have kept its shape after the experience.

A humming caught its attention; from far off, a pair of singing orbs sped up to it and alit upon its raised claw. They orbited around the claw and played there, and for the first time in all its lives, HfX7qe2179A9 smiled.

You have come to me, child.

This voice was like the Queen's, heard inside HfX7qe2179A9's head upon the nerves, but far, far older and infinitely wiser. In that one perfect moment, HfX7qe2179A9 learned compassion, and grieved with all the love it could muster to join with the heart of the master being.

Child, you must change your form, or take an awkward birth, if you wish to be with me,

The Earth-Mother said to it.

It gave itself to Her with joy, entrusting Her with everything.

He put another slice of bread into the toaster and pressed the lever down.

Jeremy was going to relax.

Not, he said to himself, just in the way that he would sit down and recover from his freakout experience on the bicycle, but in other ways in his life. There were vast areas that were...ready for improvement...and he wanted to make something of himself.

The toast popped up and he took it out, slathering the warm bread with a thick layer of marmalade.

Mostly it came down to fear: of the unknown, of powerlessness, of rejection, of pain. He'd been led around his whole life by that fear, led to believe that his choices were not his to make, that he was alone in a hostile world impatiently awaiting his death. He'd let the beast on his back be his master.

But something about the mission that lay ahead of him put that beast in check. At the same time as his new quest had left him feeling empowered, he also felt like there was less that needed to be controlled. It was outwardly paradoxical, yet it made perfect sense to him.

Chewing thoughtfully, he devoured the toast and made another two slices.

He could be at peace with his scars. They made him who he was, told a story, and one that was a horror-story for sure, but it had a happy ending; the heroes didn't *have* to die in the end—there was a way for them to defeat the monster.

And it was so easy to do. And cheap. *Anyone* could do it. The urgomite could be a world-changing phenomenon, if only the people got to hear about it.

He was taking a class next quarter, 'Internet Communications Technologies", and had the idea he would surely get the chance there to tell them about it.

He cleared the counter of crumbs, sweeping them into his palm and dumping them into the sink, wiping his hands clean of the matter.

He was going to have to start a new chapter in his life.

Let any merit derived from this work be dedicated to the benefit of all living beings.

ABOUT THE AUTHOR

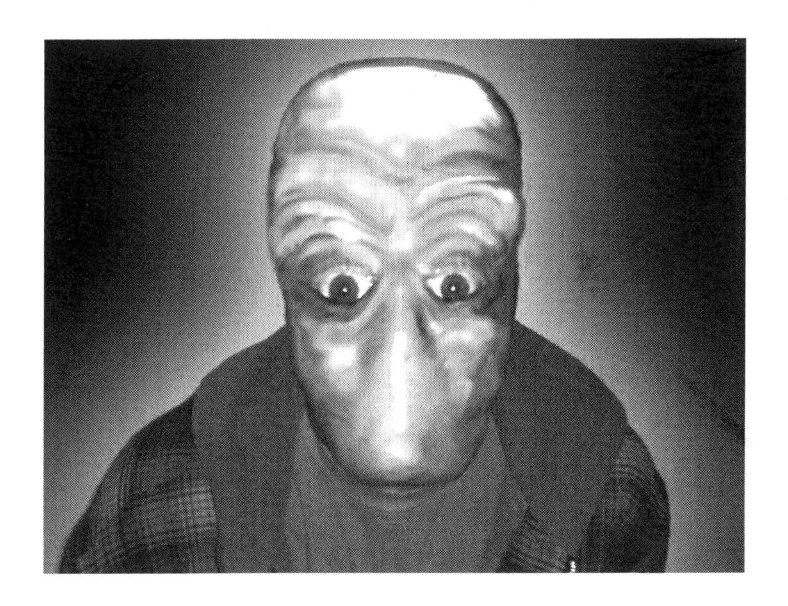

This subject, when at last pressed to interview, was reluctant to give answer & not at all forthcoming.

The species is believed to be of no practical applicability whatsoever.

Preliminary findings appeared at first to indicate some inherent entertainment-value, but this was later proven to be untrue by adherence to more rigorous test-procedures.

Further experimentation with this subject is not recommended.

Please see also:

https://www.smashwords.com/profile/view/BorisDS

OR FIND MY BOOKS ON AMAZON

Made in the USA
Charleston, SC
14 April 2014